Date
Night
Zimbell House
Anthology

Date Night

A Zimbell House Anthology

ZIMBELL HOUSE
PUBLISHING, LLC
Union Lake, MI
2017

For permission requests, write to the publisher at the address below:
"Attention: Permissions Coordinator"
Zimbell House Publishing, LLC
PO Box 1172
Union Lake, Michigan 48387
mail to: info@zimbellhousepublishing.com

© 2017 Zimbell House Publishing, LLC
Book Layout and Cover Design by *The Book Planners*
http://www.TheBookPlanner.com

Published in the United States by Zimbell House Publishing
http://www.ZimbellHousePublishing.com
All Rights Reserved

Print ISBN: 978-1-945967-07-8
Kindle ISBN: 978-1-945967-08-5
Digital ISBN: 978-1-945967-20-7
Trade Paper ISBN: 978-1-945967-59-7
Library of Congress Control Number: 2017901436

First Edition: February/2017
10 9 8 7 6 5 4

Acknowledgements

Zimbell House Publishing would like to thank all those that contributed to this anthology. We chose to showcase twelve new voices that best represented our vision for this work.

We would also like to thank our Zimbell House team for all their hard work and dedication to these projects.

Finally, a special shout-out to *The Book Planners* for creating yet another great cover design!

Contents

Art for Rookies

Maggie Veness

In the three months since I split with Samantha, I've taken off seventeen pounds and changed my shape from heavy-weight boxer to recreational gymnast. Coming straight from a shift at the hospital I find a park two blocks from the health club, scoot across to the passenger side of my sedan, and change into black tights and a baggy white tee, ready for week nine of Stretch-n-Flex.

I find Tahlia already seated on her red gym-mat. We say hi and I position my mat so I can enjoy an uninterrupted view of her every curl and crunch. Her showgirl leg extensions are remarkable. And her headstand with open-legs-split reveals a cliff and gorge that could spell the rise and fall of an entire civilization.

Today she's wearing cornflower blue tights and has her tawny curls pulled up into a high, messy knot. I don't think she knows how perfect she is. She doesn't need to make an effort like every other female on the planet.

For an hour, eighteen of us arch and contract to the best of our ability. Afterward, we hang around in our sweats, chatting over a social glass of chilled, lemon mineral water. The first time I set eyes on

Tahlia I decided she must be moving in time with some ethereal-type music we mere mortals weren't privy to hear. She doesn't exactly walk, she glides low to the ground—as if at any moment she might leap into the air like a prima ballerina.

I join a huddle of bronze-hued women and feign interest in their tips for the successful application of fake tanning products. When Tahlia glides over to join us, she smiles at me and stands so close I can count each corkscrew tendril of damp hair on her gazelle-like neck. *Seven*.

In my fleeting excursion to Fantasyland, she turns, smiling, and invites me over to her Victoria Street apartment… When she unlocks her door, I see a large, tiled entry in absolute white—white tiles, white walls, white ceiling. We move inside, and white gives way to a smattering of stainless steel—light fittings, kitchen accessories, door handles. One entire wall is covered by a stunning, ultra-modern mirror. It's a world of simple, gleaming geometry. As I follow her around the apartment, she casts off her tights and pads about, her rosy bottom as round and delicious as two strawberry cream buns.

When I re-enter the real world, people are collecting their gear and saying good-bye. A minute later I'm alone in there with Tahlia, and we're both rolling up our mats.

"So, Bonnie. What you been up to?" she asks.

"Same old. Got six shifts at the hospital this week. You?"

"Same old. Just slugging through my Arts degree. I love it, though. Did I tell you I've only got four months to go?"

"Wow! What then?"

"I've got a small job lined up at that new gallery at the Docks. I'll need time to study for my Masters so it should work out well. Hey, have you settled into that new apartment yet? 'Cause if you have you can invite me over for dinner. Theo's gone away on one of his training weeks again, and I hate eating alone night after night."

I'd dreamed that one day she'd step musically through my front door. The shock was too much. I felt some key electrical pathway deep within my brain blow a circuit and had to press my hands down on top of my head to keep it from lolling around on my shoulders.

"Shit, yeah! I mean, that'd be great. Once in a while I practically miss Samantha too, but nowhere near enough to return any of her calls if you know what I mean," I said, and the twinkle in her green eyes made me almost believe she knew I was secretly delirious in her company.

"I've got an assignment to finish tonight, Bon, but how about tomorrow night? That fit in with your shifts?"

"Too perfect. I'm on an early again tomorrow then two days off. What can I cook you?"

"Umm, I don't eat chicken, but everything else. I'll bring a nice bottle of red. Sound okay?"

I nodded up and down and tried not to hyperventilate while we exchanged phone numbers.

As I floated the two blocks back to my car, the sun was low and smudging pink and mauve above fairy-floss clouds—until a greasy-haired hulk-of-a-man wearing a brown leather bomber jacket and dirty jeans stopped to light a cigarette as I passed him on the sidewalk. I guess he liked the look of the well-muscled lycra-clad calves showing below my khaki shorts because he invited me to do something to a certain fantastically endowed part of his private anatomy—with my mouth. Anyway, I was so high about Tahlia coming over the following night that nothing else mattered and I just replied, "Nah, thanks anyway," over my shoulder and kept on floating.

With no recollection of the drive home, I entered the foyer of my building, skipped past the six ground-floor apartments, and took the checked, grey stairs two-by-two all the way up to the third floor. Along my corridor, the smoke from what smelled like charred lamb kebabs was practically thick enough to snort.

Once inside my apartment, I didn't know what to do at first because it was only twenty-five hours until Tahlia was due to arrive, so I did pogo-stick-like jumps in a figure eight around the lounge-room until I realized I could be washing all the windows.

Later, after I'd vacuumed and put every last wine glass and my dinner and cutlery sets through the dishwasher, I opened a can of Stockman's hearty beef-n-vegetable soup and warmed it on the stove, then stood watching the late show, spooning straight from the pot.

With barely nineteen hours remaining, I sat on the coffee table with a black CD marker pen and absentmindedly graffitied my left arm (with words relevant to female body worship) all the way up to my shoulder. Going to sleep, however, involved more of an intentional digital expedition as I imagined what Tahlia might want to do if she drank a little too much wine over dinner. *Hell, she may need to stay over, I told myself.* I finally fell asleep imagining a parallel universe in which Tahlia was also falling in love with me.

Sometime during the night, in a terrible dream, I was pinned down by leather-bomber-jacket-man—his filthy fingernails tearing at my clothes. The cigarette between his cruel lips glowed red in the blackness, and as I struggled to break free, he morphed into my step-father. Engulfed by searing pain, I woke up screaming for my mother. Reaching down to release my damp feet from a serious tangle of sheet, I fell back onto the bed, eventually drifting back into a restless sleep.

I clock-watched all through my morning shift, glad to be distracted first by a Spanish-speaking woman who locked herself in the ladies room and gave birth on the floor, and then by a fist-fight that broke out in the waiting room between an angry young Stallone look-alike and the guy's potty-mouth girlfriend. The brawl spread out to the parking lot and urgently required the assistance of the local cops.

All that commotion gave me a break from my lusty daydreams, such as… what if we were sitting in the lounge tonight after dinner and Tahlia confided that Theo was dead boring in bed and that she'd been thinking of taking a lover? And then what if I reached a comforting arm around her shoulders and made empathy-like noises and she turned to me and kissed my cheek but when I tried to return a likewise friendly peck… she caught it with her gorgeous full mouth and murmured… and suddenly parted her lips and started really kissing me… and her hand moved across to stroke the back of my neck as she sucked my tongue into her mouth… and then she lay back and urgently pulled me on top of her? Stuff like that.

I sped off after my shift, stopping briefly to cruise the fresh produce store and the supermarket, and arrived home with two whole hours to spare. I peeled, chopped, floured, and sautéed in a flurry, then set aside a feast. Once I'd showered and dressed, I went to wait by the bedroom window. I'd spent the previous two hours terrified she'd phone to cancel. Now I was terrified because she hadn't.

When Tahlia arrived, she breezed in wearing a small denim skirt and sleeveless, sheer yellow blouse. Her hair was loose and hung in disorganized, liquid curls way down past her shoulders. It was obvious she was braless, and for a few seconds, I felt alarmingly light-headed.

After handing me a bottle of Merlot, she tossed her tote-bag onto the coffee table, kicked off her leather sandals, then proceeded to tour my entire apartment, stopping only once to ask about the large, silver-framed Beardsley print in the lounge-room.

When I confessed I'd found it a few months back at a jumble sale, she said she thought it was stunning and a brilliant find. For a split second, I was back at that sale gushing over the print, with Samantha right next to me rolling her eyes. Too ecstatic to bother haggling, I'd pulled the ninety-five bucks from my wallet while Samantha walked off in a sulk to search for a stuffed bear to add to her collection.

"I've got a great book on Beardsley at home," said Tahlia. "I'll have to show you some time. You know, he was only twenty-five when he died. He was quite eccentric and probably Bi. As a child, he played piano and wrote poetry and drew caricatures of his teachers. Later on, he hooked up with Oscar Wilde, but that's a whole other story. A hundred years ago they called his art grotesque and perverse. I find it incredibly erotic."

I don't think there was any actual drool involved, but my mouth was definitely hanging open. Kind, graceful, smart, and stunning. I wished I could tell her how much she blew me away. I frantically searched for something intelligent to say, but all the conversations in my head began with *'I think I'm falling in love with you.'* Then her mobile rang.

"Probably Theo," she said and dug the phone out of her bag.

I returned to the kitchen so they could talk in private, then kept myself busy imagining scenarios. Maybe he'd phoned to say he was missing her so badly he'd taken an earlier flight and she was gonna have to leave immediately to collect him from the airport. Or maybe he'd won a cool million on a horse race and wondered if she'd prefer a Porsche or a Mercedes. Or maybe he'd had a nasty accident and was phoning from some hospital—about to undergo microsurgery after catching the delicate skin of his wanger on the hotel maid's dental plate wires. Those dangerous God-damn metal clasps…

Rooting for the microsurgery option, I peeped around the doorway. She was jiggling one leg and gazing at the ceiling. Was she annoyed? *Hell yeah!* She looked totally pissed! She hung up and switched off the phone, then threw it on top her bag.

"You okay?" I said.

"I guess. Every day he calls me four-five times, and even more often than that when he's away. I'm over it, Bon," she said and joined me in the kitchen. "It's getting worse, the jealousy. We've been having some awful fights. I hate to admit it, but I sort of wish he'd meet someone else on one of his trips."

"My God! I had no idea you were unhappy! Poor you," I said, already preparing my prayer of gratitude to the above-mentioned God.

"I'm not too good at choosing men. The guy I lived with before Theo turned out to be an overbearing bully, and the guy I dated before him, split with me and moved in with his forty-five-year-old violin teacher. She had a daughter my age. But that's enough about my stuff. What about you? I've been thinking about you, I mean, wondering what happened between you and Samantha."

"Umm," I said, and looked at her blankly. *Did she just say she'd been thinking about me?*

"Not that you have to tell me anything. You don't. Sorry, I shouldn't have asked."

"No, no, it's totally fine. And I'm sorry you're going through that crap with Theo," I lied. "Samantha was nice and everything, but she just got too serious too quickly. Five months together and all she could talk about was setting a date for a ceremony and having kids. She had over two hundred stuffed bears in the spare room. Big ones, little ones, pink ones, blue ones. It was starting to creep me out. Don't get me wrong. I want kids one day. I love kids."

"Me too. But what's the rush, right?" she said, and tilted her head to one side, eyes shining. And suddenly I wanted to show Tahlia all the sides of myself that I didn't even know I had. The concept of being by this woman's side to share the miracle of pregnancy and parenthood was enough to make me tear up, and I had to quickly turn away.

We drank a glass of wine while I stir-fried, and another while we ate the Moroccan lamb—which tasted damn good—all the while swapping stories and laughing across a table that she said looked all the more special for the pair of gold candles I'd lit (which made her creamy skin glisten). Eventually, we moved ourselves across onto the more comfortable sofa. While she momentarily closed her eyes and stretched her head and elbows back I got to secretly drink in the curved outline of her areolas, my eyeballs snapping back into my head when she relaxed and tucked her feet up beneath her.

There's a crucial point we all reach when we've had a couple of drinks, this being the exact moment we realize that just one more mouthful will render us powerless to lie. And there was Tahlia's bare arm brushing mine; and there was Tahlia sitting cross-legged on my sofa which had caused her short skirt to ride up and lay her smooth thighs wide open right beside me; and there was Tahlia's gorgeous long neck and that hollow at the centre of her collarbone where I just knew my warm, wet tongue would so perfectly fit.

Squirming a little, I was about to take another sip of wine when I realized I'd reached said 'crucial point.' Summoning superhuman willpower, I placed my glass on the coffee table, laced my fingers together behind my neck, closed my eyes, and took a couple of slow, controlled breaths. And that's exactly when Tahlia leaned in and draped her arm around my shoulders, and also when my eyes flew open, and I felt my pupils dilate because suddenly we were so close that I was breathing in the heady, musky aroma of her shampoo.

"Wow, you look stressy Bon. Is it your neck or your shoulders?" she said, combing her fingers through the back of my short-cropped hair. "I go for a deep tissue massage when I get tight, and it really helps," she said, then cupped her warm hand around my neck. Like her walk, Tahlia's vaguely slurred words seemed close to musical. I thought I'd pass out for sure.

"Yeah, it's, umm, my shoulders. Had a hell-of-a-shift this morning. I'll be okay."

"Please let me give you a nice, relieving rub."

And there it was: the double entendre that I knew would replay in my head every night for roughly the next sixty years.

"Oh, I couldn't expect you to do—"

"Don't be silly," she interrupted. "Let me help, Bon. Go find some oil or something then come and sit on the floor between my legs and take your t-shirt off."

Thankyouthankyouthankyou God.

My feet didn't register floor on the way to the bathroom cabinet and back. I was soon nestling down between Tahlia's legs—ergo paradise—handing over a tube of after-sun moisturizer and whipping off my shirt. As she pushed the straps of my sports bra aside, she noticed the cluster of small, circular scars on my right shoulder blade.

"How'd you get the scars?" she asked, using the tip of one finger to lightly brush over them.

"Wicked stepfather used me as an ashtray."

"Oh, Bon! That's shocking!"

"He's been dead a long time. Otherwise, I'd let you help me push him off a bridge. Some escaped looney gun-slinger thought he looked like Jeffrey Dahmer and used him for target practice."

"Sounds like divine intervention to me," she said. "So, how old were you? Did your mother know?"

I tried not to let it, but suddenly my mind flew away. My mother had gone into rehab for a month and left me in the care of my stepfather. I was ten. One evening he grabbed me and tore off my little singlet, then clamped my head face-down between his thighs while he sat smoking in his armchair. I didn't say any of this to Tahlia. These memories had always felt too fragile to expose. I would tell her. Just not now. Not when I was sitting here in Paradise. She was waiting for a reply. I shook my head. It was a tiny movement—left to right—but she understood.

"Second thoughts," she said, "let's save the gruesome details 'til some other time. Deal?"

"Deal," I said, and when she began to deftly slide her fingers back and forth along the muscles in my shoulders and neck, I thought about nothing else besides that imagined moist, pink, happy-land of nerve endings beyond the puff of dark hair between her legs.

The sound of Tahlia yawning a short while later pulled me back from my state of agonizing bliss. I lied and said she'd made all my tension vanish, thanked her, then clambered to my feet.

"No problem," she said and yawned again.

"Look, I've got a spare room, and you're welcome to stay over."

"Yeah, think I've had too much good food and wine to drive across town. I'm pretty beat. I'd better stay. Thanks, Bon."

"Too easy. Spare bed's made up. Off you go. Grab a new toothbrush from the bottom drawer in the bathroom."

"But, all the dinner dishes—"

"I'm leaving everything til tomorrow. I've got all day to clean up. Off you go. I'll find you a t-shirt or something to sleep in."

The bedside lamp was on when I entered the spare room with a t-shirt in my hand. Tahlia had just stepped out of her skirt and was standing with the back of her legs against the bed. She immediately threw off her blouse and grabbed for the t-shirt. I drew in a quick breath. For a split second, she was wearing only a teensy, black g-string. Her skin was velvet-like, her breasts small, her pale pink nipples becoming erect before my eyes. Thalia's body was more than worthy of my lusty fantasies. I transferred this extraordinary image deep into my memory bank before she pulled the t-shirt over her head.

"Night, Bon. And thanks," she said as she crawled under the doona.

"Sweet dreams," I said, my heart banging into my ribs as I flicked off the lamp.

Behind my bedroom door, I danced around the room for a minute flapping my hands and making faces like a lunatic at full moon, then threw off my clothes and fell onto the bed. I thought about Tahlia's near naked body in the next room and imagined lying beside her, my lips forming a warm, wet ring around each of her nipples before drawing them into my mouth, her moans guiding my hand lightly across her smooth belly, slowly stroking the inside of her velvety thighs, eventually seeking out her swollen folds of slippery warmth. And very soon my back was arching with waves of intense pleasure that rolled me toward a deep, restful sleep.

By the time I surfaced at around eight the next morning, Tahlia had gone. She'd left a thank-you note that said she'd really enjoyed our girl's night and was looking forward to me coming to her place for dinner next time Theo went away. I carried that note around in my pocket all day; pulled it out to re-read it maybe twenty times.

Over the following days, the memory of her presence within my apartment was a shimmering mirage that never settled. The idea of Tahlia's forthcoming invitation sat like a seed planted far too early in the season—just beneath my conscious mind waiting for nature to take its place. Soon I was pacing around the apartment like some pathetic, love-struck teenager. I was desperately in need of distraction. By the third day, an idea came to mind—something I imagined would give me some reprieve. After an hour of online research, I found myself driving to the city with a pocket full of cash.

★★★★

For the next seven weeks, I counted the days down between our Stretch-n-Flex class, hanging out for the brief but brilliant chat and brief but brilliant hug we'd share afterward. While Tahlia had confessed to being unhappy with Theo, I was forced to acknowledge that she chose to stay with him. In a bid to keep my mind off her, I took to cycling and swimming laps at the local pool, but falling exhausted into bed each night changed nothing. My chest ached for her, and I'd often cry myself to sleep. Fact was, I'd fallen for someone I could never be with, and I was slowly losing my mind.

Then, seven weeks after she'd joined me for dinner, Tahlia delivered some hellish sweet news. Theo was going away. And with her dinner invitation, the black clouds parted. Once again my sky was smudging pink.

★★★★

With all that cycling and swimming I've lost another eight pounds. I'm feeling fit and taut. I'm at Tahlia's for dinner, and we've just shared a delicious seafood hot-pot and a bottle of Pinot Noir.

"I've got something to show you. Bought it a few weeks back," I say.

"What is it?"

"You gotta guess."

"Okay. Did you buy a new car?"

"Nope."

"Hmm. You bring it with you?"

"Yep."

"Is it in your bag?"

"Nope."

"Then it has to be in your pocket. A new phone?"

"Not a phone, no."

"Hmmmmm. I reckon you've been to another jumble sale only this time you've found a miniature treasure. A piece of art. Am I right?"

"Not exactly."

"Ooooh. I'm getting warmer. It's an artwork of some kind, right?" she says, one eyebrow lifting.

"Maybe. But no jumble sale this time."

"So you bought an artwork?" she says, her back straightening against the padded dining chair.

"Well, I guess you could say that."

"And you have it with you?"

"I've got it with me, yeah," I say, and watch her eyes flick over the pockets of my jeans. I can't help but smile. "But it's not in my pocket."

"Well, where is it? I give up."

"Already? But this is fun!" I say. She's frowning now, folding her arms and making an exaggerated pout.

"Come on, Bon!"

"Okay, you win." I stand quickly and step clear of the table. Turning away, I whip off my t-shirt and reveal the tattoo trailing down from my right shoulder blade all the way to my waist.

"Maison Roos! It's Beardsley's Maison Roos!" she cries.

The striking black figure, wearing a sweeping full-length peacock dress, perfectly depicts Beardsley's trademark intricately decorative style. "Seemed like a positive way to cover some ugly scars," I tell the wall opposite.

"It's beautiful, Bon! And the scars have vanished. I love tattoos! God, it must have hurt. It's huge! I'd never be brave enough. Okay if I touch?"

"Sure. It's completely healed," I say, and try to calm my racing pulse.

Flattening her palm, she skims over my tattoo from shoulder to waist, then flips me around for a huge hug. And suddenly my bare chest is hard against Tahlia's white, cotton shirt and my mind spins out into the cosmos. Then I feel one of her hands sliding down my back, and freeze. It's moving so lightly and sensually that I don't know how or even if I'm meant to react. Pulling back a little, she drops her head and stares at the space between our feet.

"I… I don't know how, umm, I don't know what to, I mean…"

"Yes you do," I say, and touch my lips to her forehead. My heart is pumping with fast, sickening beats.

When she looks up, my mouth nervously brushes hers. She parts her lips, and we fall inside a shy kiss. I'm in a state of joyful delirium. Then she offers me her tongue, and I can't help but moan. I don't want this to go wrong. I don't want to rush her or frighten her or do anything she doesn't like, so I do nothing else. I just keep kissing her. A few moments later her hands edge around to my ribcage then gradually slide upward to nervously explore my breasts.

Just like mine, Tahlia's breathing rate has doubled. I take a chance and trail light kisses across her cheek to her jaw, then use my tongue to find that sweet hollow at the base of her slender neck, all the while, fumbling to unbutton her shirt. Her whole body is trembling. Very softly, my hand moves down over her belly, and I hear her inhale sharply. My warm, wet mouth leaves her neck to seek out her erect nipples.

"Oh, God," she whispers. "I want this so much. You. I want you so much."

Feeling the prick of tears, I mumble, "You've known all along, haven't you, that I've fallen in love with you."

She answers with an urgent kiss. Suddenly she's pushing me away and grabbing me by the hand and leading me across the room to lie down with her on the low, velvet chaise. Ergo, paradise.

Counting Coins

Elizabeth Abeling

I throw my keys in the bowl on the mantle like I'm returning home. They make a swishing ceramic noise, and Jason's tepid "Hello?" answers like an echo from the next room.

"Hey," I answer, pulling awkwardly at my boots. I see a pile of shoes by the door and laugh; he's made it one of those houses, where socks whisper across floors without clunking soles, dirt, and salt confined to a sweepable, manageable corner.

We used to make fun of those people, those houses—so stuffy, so worried about appearances. I decide my shoes are tied too tightly to bother with, and take a few steps into the room, leaving my bag on the table by the door. "It's freezing out there," I yell, probably a little too loudly.

"Yeah," he yells back. I hear footsteps but they're going the other way, and by the time I enter the dining room he's gotten to the kitchen. A disembodied voice asks me if I want a beer.

"Thanks," I answer, pushing in a chair, listening to the odd squeal of wood and friction. I don't sit down; I pace.

When he enters the room again he's not carrying a beer, and there's a part of me that knows it's intentional, but I let him have this one. He sits down at the behemoth of a dining room table, all solid oak, stretching the vastness of the room.

He sits at the head because of course, he does. He's cleared a seat off a reasonable, palatable distance from him, just a chair or two down. I move a pile of clothes and take the seat next to him. My jacket's still on. Something about it is comforting. Another layer of insulation.

The coin jar is sitting in the middle of the table, plopped there like an ugly centerpiece. We'd planned this for months. Maybe a year.

Well, we never got to it.

We'd both grown this fascination with the coin jar, tracking its growth, making guesses at its weight and value. It hung in the room like we were waiting for the raffle results for one of those how-many-jelly-beans carnival games. We fed it daily, pocket change tossed like a ritual, like a habit.

It took our proffered coins, and it grew. We'd take handfuls, run the metal through our fingers like we'd stopped touching each other, and needed something to touch. We'd listen to the rustling like it could tell us something.

Anything.

We needed to know. The bank or the Coin Star would tell us, but there was something visceral about the touch of those coins, something pulling at us.

We planned this night like most couples would plan a date. I don't think he really expected me to keep it, after everything, but I'm committed. I think I even planned an outfit.

I don't know what I thought it would sound like when all those coins hit the table, watching that river of metal, like slow motion flowing out of the jar. Like love, like mourning. Like a waterfall or an avalanche.

An earthquake.

Windstorms.

Cracking ice.

Well. It sounded like coins on wood.

"Fuck," says Jason, when it's all said and done, that metal sea stretching between us. The mass of coins—it looked bigger, out of the jar. "I never got you that beer," he says.

I laugh, but he doesn't ask what's funny. "I'll get it," I say. I was always going to get it.

The kitchen is bright, sunlight sneaking easy and soft through the window, showering the white tile floor with a glare. The fridge holds most of a case, but there's not much else, maybe a few scattered take-out containers. Half a can of tuna sits in a ziplock bag, and the vegetables I'd bought three months ago are still rotting in the crisper drawer.

I take the vegetables out and toss the bags in the trash. Trash day was yesterday, and he'll have to live with the smell for a bit, but hey, it was overdue.

I throw away his tuna too because he knows I hate it.

The swinging lid on the trash can crashes closed, and my muddy boots echo the reverberation back into the dining room.

His ears prick up, and I wonder how long it will take him to ask me to remove my shoes.

Jason's picked quarters. He has them lined up in rows like infantrymen, perfect stacks of four in perfect rows of five. He wants this to go quickly. He'll probably try to skip the pennies.

I start with the pennies. I won't make this easy.

We share the brief courtesy of silence. It's a good two minutes at least before it becomes uncomfortable, before his tapping fingers sound like snare drums.

I want to tell him, "Stop."

I want to scream it.

I am at fifty-six pennies, past the halfway point on the long highway to a dollar, and under the guise of rifling for more, I can drown him, briefly.

When I hit seventy pennies I don't think of drowning him so literally anymore; it's all just noise and light and numbers counting up and down in my head.

At eighty pennies he's barely a thought, his tapping fingers functioning as a backbeat to my rifling. I start tapping with him; we synthesize; it's almost orchestral.

He stops tapping and sips. A pile of quarters sits unsorted in front of his ordered ranks, but his arm reaches into the pile to sift for more. The clatter cuts through my tapping. My rhythm's gone; the seven pennies in my hand are sifted, counted, sifted, counted again.

I will never get to ten like this.

He asks again if I want a beer and it's only then that I realize I never got one from the fridge, the heaping trashcan the only evidence I'd been through at all, too intent on my vegetable purge to get what I came for.

Out with the old, in with the eighty-something cents.

It's weird, for me, to forget proffered free drinks. I glare; I count with determination; I place, defiantly, a stack of ten copper soldiers.

Ninety pennies.

I grab a beer. I toy with throwing out his take-out too, but I open it first and see a thin layer of mold gathering on his General Tso's. It can stay.

My jacket rustles uncomfortably in the silence, a washboard scratch on his shuffled off-beat.

I kick the cap off the beer with my lighter. Sure, there's a wine key in my pocket, and we have bottle openers—no, he has bottle openers, second drawer from the sink, to the right—but I know it annoys him when I do that. The pop of the cap is different somehow, the prying of metal from glass fiercer, the pressure release just barely more forceful.

Or maybe it's all in his head.

I try to make it as loud as I can, but in the trying something snags. My hand slips and the flap of skin between my thumb and pointer is left—well, not deep enough to bleed, but raggedy, and it smarts, and I mutter "Fuck," and his army of quarters grows.

My pennies don't stand a chance.

I glare a little—a warning glance.

"Are you going to need a ride home?" he asks.

He's trying to sound nonchalant, but he's already thinking about me going home. I take off my jacket. Hell, I might even untie my shoes.

I won't take them off, but I might untie them.

We will sit and count these coins until they tell us something, or at least until they are gone. I'm not going to give up on that feeling, on holding that metallic knowledge in my hands. If it's the last thing we do together, I will take measure, inch by inch, penny by penny, of whatever is left of us.

He's looking at me, eyebrow raised, tapping a solitary quarter against the oak, scratching the finish. I sit down. If I can hold off answering long enough, my pennies might catch up.

I think about the hour-long bus ride and the crying child who spent the whole time kicking the seat behind mine. I think about my broken headphones, how only the one earbud works, the wobbly off-balance feeling it gives me to listen to anything at all. I think about the smell of the 16 bus, and the sketchy bus stop by his house, the bullet holes in the payphone by the sign.

"I'll be fine," I say. Fuck if I'm getting into a car with him when our whole house feels this small.

His house.

He looks relieved, sighs like pressure escaping from his chest.

"But I guess I wouldn't say no," I tell him.

One hundred pennies stand in perfect stacks of ten.

When we first moved in, we didn't do it box-by-box. We picked and chose small things; a poster here, an end table there. We selected, first, what we knew we wanted—whatever was fit for display. For guests. For company.

We made it look like a proper home, debating at length about the worth of our wall art, the placement of our meager furniture. After all, we had all this time to move in. 'We have forever,' he'd said with a smile, his hands twisting at the ring around my finger.

It made it very easy for me when I was leaving. Most of my things were still in boxes, tucked into shelves or packed neatly in the basement like infantrymen, perfect stacks of four in perfect rows of five.

Jason triumphantly stacks the last of forty-three piles of quarters, but as he reaches for dimes, he uncovers a hidden cove in the still-massive pile, covered by a penny cascade.

His foot taps like an impatient child, and I stop counting.

"I need to stretch my legs," I say. He taps faster. He grunts. Nods. Like I need his permission.

A lamp sits in the corner of the room, shaped like a covered wagon. It looks like something you got when Grandma died, and you can't just throw it away, Mom says, 'well fine, you keep it, then.' It looks like what happens when drunken antique shopping goes wrong.

I'd lifted it from the curb years before, salvaged it from a pile of rotting doilies atop a box inexplicably marked nicknacks. Jason loved this lamp. Jason was eyeing this lamp as I prowled the dining room, opening boxes to see what was mine.

They were all mine, of course, but Jason had packed them so neatly with this stupid expensive packing tape of his, and it ripped so easily with the blade of the two-dollar wine key I kept in my back pocket.

I touch the lamp, brushing a bit of dust from its dented shade, and a pile of quarters slams on the table with just barely too much force.

Even if I have to carry it by myself on the bus, crushing my lap while a gaggle of small children squirms uncomfortably in the seat next to me, broken headphones blaring half a song, I am taking the damn lamp, and I am doing it tonight.

I sit again and count out a few piles in silence, and every time I look up, his eyes are darting to the lamp. I smile and stack my soldiers.

At two hundred pennies, the silence gets to me, and I decide it's time to smoke, slipping back into my jacket. I head through the kitchen to the back door.

"Grab me a beer on your way back?" he asks.

"Sure," I say. I won't.

Outside is still chilly, but the sun has spent the day warming the spots of the yard that aren't cast in shadow.

He's cleaned out all the ashtrays since I've left.

I squat on the end of one of the lounge chairs his parents picked out last summer, floral print over dark-stained wicker. A few of my abandoned lighters are sitting on the shelf nearby where he keeps the ashtrays and the grill tongs. I test one; it still works. I light my smoke and pocket it.

It wasn't supposed to be like this. But every couple says that, don't they?

We cried together when it ended, held each other in the dining room, my tears soaking the shoulder of his flannel shirt. "It'll be okay," he told me, hand moving circular on my spine like comfort. "We can still be friends."

That should have been the first clue.

"You don't get it," I told him.

"Don't get what?"

I pulled away, wiped my tears from my face, smiling broadly, eyes shining. "I'm so happy," I said. "I'm so. Fucking. Happy."

He looked hurt, and I couldn't understand why.

"Don't you see?" I asked. "We never were friends. We can finally be fucking friends."

He smiled, then. But I don't think he really meant it.

When I come inside, he's standing in front of the open fridge, taking out a beer. He moves to the drawer to extract a bottle opener.

"I'd have gotten that for you," I say, and he laughs. "What's so funny?"

"Nothing," he tells me.

The pennies are all but counted, four-hundred-twelve, with a few copper flecks hiding in the sea of silver. No use fishing for them when they'll reveal themselves in the rummaging, so I start with nickels.

They're too thin to stack in twenties, too unwieldy, toppling with the slightest bustle of Jason's growing field of dimes. I settle for stacks of ten. Table space is growing scarcer, so I have them meander through my ranks of pennies, twisting pathways around the ordered lines.

Jason's laid out a sheet of paper and a pen, to tally the piles, to count our hoard.

I won't use the tallies, and he's beginning to glare.

I grab another beer.

When I come back, he's poking at my piles, marking them off on his orderly sheet. His mouth is moving, counting silently up and down.

"So what've you been up to lately?" I ask, flicking at my lighter as I maneuver its base against the cap. He bites his lip and closes his eyes as I pry the cap off.

"I lost count," he says.

"Exciting life," I say, but he doesn't get the joke.

I take my seat and place the beer bottle squarely on his tally marks. He clicks his pen in a way that's almost menacing. I lean back in my chair and raise an eyebrow.

"No really," I say. "What's your life like right now?"

Now that he's not answering, I almost want to know.

"Listen," he starts, and now I don't want to.

Again, I raise an eyebrow. The way he's looking at me, it's like it was that night with the crying, a look that says this could take a while.

"I think this should be the last time we see each other," he says. "I think it's better to leave the past in the past."

We can finally be friends, I think, like an echo of someone else. I stare for a long time at the piles of coins dotting the table. I wonder if he expects me to cry. *It'll be okay,* I remember.

"I can help you move over the rest of your stuff," he says.

You don't get it, I think.

"I don't want a consolation prize," I tell him. I take a hearty swig of beer and slam the bottle on the table. The carbonation makes for a cascade effect, bubbles frothing upward like a children's model volcano, lava soaking his tallies, spilling over the table's edge.

I guess I'm glad I never took off my shoes.

"What do you want, then?" he asks. His voice is raised, but it still sounds like a genuine question, like he maybe really wants an answer.

"I want my fucking lamp," I tell him, and head to the corner. I remove the lampshade and tuck the body of it under my arm, the material a weighty ceramic too heavy to carry comfortably, but I won't let him see that.

"I'm trying to be civil," he tells me.

"By asking me what I want?" I laugh. "Here, let me rip your fucking heart out, but I'm civil because I asked what you wanted after. Civil. Fuck you, what do I want. I want to be in your life. I want to be your friend."

Jason laughs and shakes his head.

"What's so fucking funny?"

"We were never really friends," he says.

I pull my bag from the chair and swing it over my shoulder. "Sure," I say. "Use that against me now. Do you even remember what I said next?"

"Why does it matter?" he yells, hands gripping his hair like he's about to rip it out.

"Just text me the number, okay?" I tell him. "That's what I want."

"What number?"

"Just tell me how much was in the jar. I'll come get my shit next week while you're at your parents'. No need for us to talk."

He steps forward, his face softening a little, and there's something about the angle of the chair when his hip knocks it, something about the placement of those last few nickels, and I hear a cavalcade of copper soldiers toppling behind me, piles crashing, uncounted, unrecorded.

Domino effect.

His army falls to the floor, and it sounds like nothing.

Jason says something, but I don't really want to hear him, so I don't. I keep walking, and there's his hand on my shoulder, and I bristle, and there goes the damn lamp. I watch it fall, feel the last of its weight slip from where it was tucked under my elbow, and the crash drowns out anything Jason was trying to yell, anyway.

I listen to it like it can tell me something.

Like a waterfall, an avalanche. An earthquake. Like love, like mourning.

A little like coins on wood.

Couples Night

Paul Lewellan

I wasn't looking forward to the evening, but Elaine and I ran out of excuses for not getting together with the Griffins. Aaron Griffin and I had worked together at First Midwestern Charter Bank for almost a decade. I headed the Investment Management group. He was senior VP for the Loan division. Three years ago he found God. Aaron had apparently been looking for Him for some time.

He cut back to a two-thirds time so he could take classes evenings, weekends, and on-line at a small Bible college an hour's commute from Mount Union. Aaron used his accrued vacation time to do an internship at a prospering church in Raleigh, North Carolina. The pastor there was someone he'd met on a mission trip.

"The congregation offered me the associate pastor's job as soon as they heard me preach," he humbly explained upon his return to work. "But God is calling me here to the river." Three weeks later the freshly ordained Reverend Aaron Griffin opened a storefront ministry in downtown Mount Union.

"Apparently there aren't enough churches in Iowa already," my wife snickered when she heard about it.

"Nine people attended his first bible study," I told Elaine as she sipped on a glass of Trimbach Riesling. An offer had just fallen through on a high-end condo she'd been pitching, and she was consoling herself. "He seemed elated."

"His relations were probably two-thirds of the attendees," she sneered. "But I know for a fact his wife wasn't one of them. Connie had a showing in the Broadview Addition."

My wife, Elaine, was the top selling home real estate agent in our two-state region, four of the last seven years. Aaron's wife, Connie, was the top agent the other three years. The two women were competitive.

Elaine came from a real estate family, but choose not to remain at her father's firm after we married. In contrast, Connie began her career selling auto insurance for State Farm but shifted to real estate when she moved to Mount Union because of Aaron's bank job.

Connie was a fast study and a strikingly attractive redhead. She ran track at Boise State, qualifying for the NCAA Championships in the 800 meters her senior year. She was also Miss Boise and finished second runner-up in the Miss Idaho pageant.

In the span of eleven months, Aaron's congregation, Jesus at the Door Christian Church, changed storefronts three times, outgrowing each space within weeks of moving in. When the church council made an offer to buy a closed parochial school from the local Catholic diocese, Aaron cut back to half time at the bank.

"There aren't enough hours in the day," he told me one day before a meeting. By Thanksgiving, he planned to quit banking altogether.

Initially, our wives worked for competing real estate firms, but two weeks ago Elaine came home and announced that her agency had been bought out by Connie's. "John, she could be my boss."

So when Aaron asked if Elaine and I were free Friday night, I said yes. "Why don't you bring an appetizer and dessert," he told me. "I'm taking the afternoon off to fix beef bourguignon and a French onion soup. Connie will make a salad."

When I got home from the bank Friday afternoon, I found Elaine in the kitchen making sweet and spicy jalapeno poppers. "When was the last time you baked?" I commented. "I thought you were going to buy a shrimp platter from Red Lobster and a pie from Village Inn."

"If that bitch is cooking, I'm cooking," my ultra-competitive wife told me.

Actually, I knew Aaron was the cook in the Griffin family but didn't want to start an argument.

"What's for dessert?"

Elaine pointed to the kitchen counter. "I made a Coconut-Pecan German Chocolate Pie."

That's when I caught a glimpse under her robe. "What are you wearing?"

Elaine finished plating the poppers and pretended she hadn't heard me. When she turned back to face me, her robe came undone, and my worst suspicions were confirmed.

"Let me see."

My wife shrugged the silk robe off her shoulders revealing the matching red lace bustier, thong, and banded garter slip she'd bought last Valentine's Day to surprise me.

"Garters. Really?" I asked.

"To hold up the seamed nylons from Fredrick's." She motioned to the Fed Ex envelope on the counter.

"Don't get me wrong, Elaine, I'm excited about the possibilities here, but we've got dinner plans with a freshly minted minister and his wife. You're dressed to turn tricks on Second Street."

"Now, John, you know Second Street men couldn't afford me." She noted the exasperated look on my face. "Actually, I hoped to play more than a game of Bible Trivia this evening."

"With the Griffins?"

"No. Of course not! Although Aaron is a handsome man." Elaine eased over, stroked my arm gently, and purred. "I thought we could cut the evening short, then go out for a late night drink."

My wife is an exhibitionist. We used to frequent out-of-the-way bars and clubs so she could role-play. But we hadn't done that in years, certainly not since she topped the real estate charts, and her company plastered her image on all their billboards.

"Besides," she reassured me, "I want to make sure I keep your attention as the night wears on."

Although she'd never admit to being jealous, Elaine had frequently commented on Connie's tendency to wear tight skirts and low cut blouses. "Business acumen isn't her best asset," she'd told me. Again I didn't argue.

"I'm going to wear jeans."

"I'd prefer your new Cesare Attolini sport coat and slacks."

"Definitely not."

"Then how about the Hilfiger? Oxford shirt. No tie."

"Why should I wear anything but jeans and a polo shirt?"

"Because you want me naked at the end of the evening." Elaine picked up her robe and started walking to the bedroom. "And that's not going to happen if you wear jeans."

I wore my light blue sport coat.

Aaron met us at the door and asked what we'd like to drink. Apparently drinking alcohol wasn't a problem in his church. He made Elaine a gin and tonic with Hendrick's and a cucumber slice. I got a Dorothy's New World lager, while Aaron opened a Viña Polkura Syrah Marchigue for himself. "Connie went for a run and lost track of time."

As if on cue, Aaron's wife burst through the door in running shorts, ratty tank top, and a sweat-drenched sports bra. "I'll pop into the shower and throw on some clothes..." she saw us and stopped. She looked at her watch. "Shit."

She turned to her husband. "Sorry. I thought you said six-thirty." She looked over to Elaine in her simple black dress. "I'd better change." She saw me in my sport coat. She turned back to her husband. "Maybe you should, too." He was in Polo jeans and an oxford shirt.

"I'm fine." Aaron raised his wine glass and drank. Connie didn't contradict him. She rushed off to shower.

By the time she rejoined us in the living room, we were all on our second drink. She'd traded her running shoes for three-inch heels. Her tan pencil skirt ended mid-thigh, but it was the cleavage exposed by her blue satin blouse that made the outfit pop. I speculated on Connie's undergarments.

Aaron handed her a Jim Beam single barrel bourbon and rocks. A double.

Over drinks and Elaine's jalapeno poppers, we fell into easy conversation until suddenly I was struck by the silence of the house. "Where are the kids?"

"They're with their grandparents," Connie told me. "We thought we'd have more fun if we had the house to ourselves."

"And on that note," Aaron announced, "dinner is served in the dining room."

He ladled out four bowls of hot French onion soups, topped each with thin, crisp rounds of bruschetta and a slice of Swiss cheese melted with a culinary torch at the table. The soup was followed by Connie's contribution, a seven-layer salad purchased at Costco. That was followed by Aaron's beef bourguignon. "You can't go wrong," he told us, "using Julia Child's recipe."

Conversation drifted from bank business to Aaron's new church, and finally the upcoming real estate office merger. The women warmed to the prospect of working together, but maybe it was the alcohol talking.

"So," I asked after we'd moved to the family room, "why didn't we do this a long time ago?"

"This?" Connie asked, settling into her favorite loveseat.

"Have a couples night," Aaron suggested.

Elaine laughed. "Because we've always hated each other."

Connie demurred. "Not hatred really. We are more like rivals."

I protested. "Aaron and I aren't—"

"Of course we are, John. The Board has always played us off each other, dangling performance incentives, keeping us on tight leashes." Connie snickered at the word 'leashes.' She tugged at her short skirt, and then glanced up to catch me staring.

Aaron leaned back on the green couch next to the stone fireplace. Connie was seated beside him, angled toward me. I sat on the maroon loveseat opposite them.

Elaine faced Aaron, and when she was sure she had his attention, she crossed her legs. The lace tops of her nylons became visible with hints of the garters attached to them. She took another sip of gin, and then closed her eyes and listened as Aaron spoke.

"My desire to start a church was driven by God, but also by a desire to loose the tether. And when you become the next bank president, a weight will be lifted." He raised his wine glass to salute me. The glass was overfull, and he spilled some on his jeans. "Once in charge, you'll make your mark in this community."

I sat up on the loveseat. "You're already changing things: your storefront ministry, the bible studies, community outreach, social action..." But then I got it, what he was trying to tell me. I raised my beer glass. "To us."

"Rivals forever," he slurred.

We drank.

Elaine set down her empty glass and turned to Connie. "Frankly, I never realized you so devoted?"

Aaron's wife snorted an unladylike response. "Who said I'm religious?"

"Well, I assumed..." Elaine feared she'd lost track of the conversation.

Connie leaned toward her, a motion that flashed her breasts and the sheer camisole that barely covered them.

"I grew up in an orthodox Catholic household. Protocol had to be followed. My parents demanded that my sisters and I follow strict rules. We had to dress our best, and above all, we had to obey. Well, I got tired of that shit." My wife nodded as though she understood. "I attended Boise State because it was as close to the End of the Earth as my controlling parents would allow."

"Is that where you met Aaron?"

"No, we met in a playgroup after college while I was selling insurance."

"A play group?" Suddenly my senses were tingling. "What kind of play group?"

"Adult," she said coyly. "We met when a public dungeon in Spokane hosted an open house weekend. My boss at the agency in Boise offered to fly me there in his private plane."

My wife's eyes were wide open at this point. "A dungeon?"

"BDSM, I assume." I looked to Connie for confirmation.

"Yes. I'd experimented some with hot wax and a little cutting, but that wasn't my thing. My boss suggested the Cheshire Cat Club would be a safe way to explore my—"

"—Proclivities," Aaron offered. "I was living in Portland at the time. I was one of the regulars."

"The setup was pretty basic," Connie explained, "a corridor of cages, Saint Andrew's crosses in varied sizes, a stage with a mirrored backdrop, a refreshment bar, and a small gift store that sold whips, ropes, dildos, leather restraints, and ball gags. There was costume rental."

"For Open House Weekends, penetration and alcohol are prohibited," Aaron added.

Elaine took all this in with wide-eyed wonder.

"One of the charter members told me I'd know what I wanted when I saw it." Connie laughed. "And I did," she said, looking right at her husband.

Aaron grinned proudly. "I was giving a caning demonstration on the main stage when I caught her eye."

"He had a woman tied to a table with white cotton ropes. It excited me in ways I had never imagined."

"Connie volunteered for the 9 p.m. show."

"I quickly realized it wasn't the caning I craved, but rather the bondage. I wanted to give up control, to let a man have his way with me."

"A rape fantasy," Elaine offered.

"No. Not at all. It was about power, mine and his." Connie bent down to pick up her empty bourbon glass and caught me staring again. "When you tie up a stranger to force sex—that is rape." She walked over to the loveseat and picked up our empty glasses. "This is different." She took the glasses to the bar. "*Bondage makes sex better for both of you.*"

"The bondage required you to give yourself up completely," Aaron added.

"I can't do that," my wife told him. "And frankly I'm a little surprised to hear this coming from you, *Pastor* Griffin."

"It's biblical," he explained. "Ephesians 5:22–26 taken to its logical conclusion."

"Oh, please," Elaine said and folded her arms in front of her as if the discussion was over.

"No, I'd like to hear this," I said.

Connie returned and stood beside her husband, listening, although I figured she'd heard this before.

"In Ephesians 5:22, Saint Paul wrote his blueprint for a Christian marriage." As Aaron explained, Connie stroked his shoulder. Her eyes, though, were focused on me. "'Wives, submit to your husbands as to the Lord.'" She leaned over and nibbled his ear.

"Stop that," Aaron hissed. He pushed her away. "This is important."

"I know, dear." Connie moved toward me. "You want Elaine to understand."

I looked to Aaron and followed his gaze to my wife, now alert, perhaps even… aroused.

"In verse 24 Saint Paul urged, 'as the church submits to Christ, so wives should submit to their husbands in everything.'"

"'In everything,'" I echoed, but Elaine wasn't listening to me. "Nothing wrong with a little bondage," I told Connie, standing beside me. "It's Biblical."

"No one is tying me up," my wife said firmly. She'd begun to perspire. "That's not what Saint Paul meant by submission."

I could feel the heat emanating from Connie's body. I was getting a little warm myself.

"On the contrary, he wrote in I Corinthians 9:27, 'I beat my body and bring it into submission.'" My wife unfolded her arms. Her hands dropped to her lap, tense, anticipatory, her fingers splayed against the fabric of her simple black dress.

"Bondage excites me in ways nothing else does," Connie explained as she stroked my neck. "When I surrender myself, I can release." For a moment we were frozen in a tableau.

Aaron finally broke the silence. "Tell me, Elaine, why did you dress the way you did tonight?"

"It had nothing to do with you," she said defensively. "We planned to leave early and find a bar."

"Somewhere you weren't known?"

"Yes."

"To do anonymously, things that excite you?"

"Yes."

"You don't need to leave to do that," Aaron said. "Stand up. I'll show you."

Elaine's flushed. "I beg your pardon?"

"My husband told you to stand up," Connie interjected. "Don't make him ask again."

"Why not?"

I knew the answer. "Because you'd have to be punished," I suggested.

"What?" Elaine looked up at me, surprised.

"John is exactly right," Aaron assured her. "How did you know that?"

"Because that's what I'd want to do."

"Punish her?"

"Definitely." By now my wife's rival, Connie, had unbuttoned my shirt and begun stroking my chest." Only then did Elaine understand, and smile.

"Stand up," Aaron repeated.

She did as she was told.

"Take off the dress."

She reached behind her back, warning me off when I reached to help with the zipper. She eased the straps off first one shoulder, then the next, slowly, deliberately, and seductively. As Connie's hand moved to the front of my slacks, Elaine pushed the dress past her ample hips and let it fall in a pool on the floor, revealing her red bustier and thong, the banded garter slip, seamed nylons, and stiletto heels.

Aaron stood for a long time admiring her. Silent. Deliberate. "Yes," he said finally, "you have done well."

Only then did she turn from me to him. "Thank you."

Aaron relaxed, but only for an instant. "From this point on," he said firmly, "you should speak only when spoken to."

She nodded.

"So, you're in charge?" I asked.

"Only if you two agree. I will be the Dominant on our couples nights."

After noting the use of the plural noun, Elaine and I consented.

"I suspect, John, that you are a Top. You're used to taking charge but are not averse to giving up control if the situation is right. Your beautiful wife, Elaine, clearly is a Bottom, forced to take charge sometimes, especially in the outer world, but willing to surrender herself for the chance of greater pleasure."

"And what are you?" I asked Connie.

Aaron signaled for his wife to stop stroking me. He motioned for her to stand beside him. "My wife is one of the lucky few we call a Switch. She moves effortlessly between the roles. When she came into the Portland BDSM scene, she was in great demand. And not just for her obvious attributes. It's an indulgence we lost when we moved here."

Elaine's face was awash with emotions, but she remained silent. "Do you have something to say?" Aaron asked her.

"What happens on Bible Study nights? Is your church a sex club?"

Aaron laughed long and hard at that. "No. That's nonsense. My church, its mission, its commitment to service and social justice is the real thing. We serve free community meals on Sunday nights and have opened a food pantry. We are planning a shelter for homeless teens. But in a way, the church is also the reason we invited you two here tonight."

"I understand."

"Then explain it to me, John," Elaine sputtered, "because I don't."

"The church's success has made Aaron more visible," I said, "more of a public figure, under more scrutiny than in the past. It's made him vulnerable to criticism." That's when the logic of the evening struck me. "We're vulnerable, too, Elaine. That's why we stopped going to those clubs. Everyone recognizes you from the real estate ads."

"The new owners want us to do TV spots together," Connie explained to Elaine, "like Rizzoli and Isles. There will be no place we can go anonymously."

"Any indiscretion," Aaron said, "caught on a stranger's cell phone camera, could destroy your career and your husband's."

"If you need to give in to your desires, do it with people like us," Connie offered, "who have as much to lose as you do. People you can trust."

"Bondage is all about trust." Aaron reached out to my wife. "Are you ready to trust me?" Elaine took his hand. "For your protection, we'll need to establish some rules, hard and soft limits, perimeters, safe words." He began to lead her out of the family room. "Let me show you our private place."

"Where's he taking her?" I asked Connie.

"Aaron built a small dungeon in our basement, where his workshop used to be." And then the inevitable question hung in the air until she finally asked me. "Are you ready?"

I grinned. "I am."

"Then strip," Connie commanded. "Tonight, I own you." Before I could object, she added. "Next time, you can be in charge." She wrinkled her nose playfully at me.

"That sounds fair."

I removed my Hilfiger jacket and chinos, my oxford shirt, boxers, shoes, and socks. As Connie led me to the dungeon to play, she explained the rules, and so began our first couples night.

Date Night

Joe Sifton

Simon was drinking far too quickly, and he knew it. A large glass of wine like this should have lasted much longer. Instead, it was nearly empty after just five minutes. He couldn't stop looking around, scanning the room to see if she'd arrived yet. Not that she'd be on time, of course, it was only just after eight now. He'd been here since a quarter to eight, sitting in the sumptuous hotel restaurant, wondering what he was doing in a place like this, feeling he didn't belong. The voice in his head kept telling him this was madness, that this wasn't the sort of thing he usually did. He felt that any minute he was going to give in to those thoughts, lose his nerve and walk out. *No,* said another, much calmer voice. *Sit tight, drink your wine, relax. You're going to see this through, you know you want to.*

He ran his fingers through his thinning hair, realized what he was doing and stopped. It was starting to become a habit, and the last thing he needed was to draw attention to his bald patch. Not that there was anything he could do about it, he just had to hope she didn't notice it. But that was a stupid thought, of course, she'd notice it, he just had to hope she didn't mind. Perhaps he wouldn't keep worrying about it if they hadn't seated him right opposite that huge mirror? Every time he looked up he couldn't help seeing himself reflected in it—a man the wrong side of forty, looking as if he didn't belong, losing his hair, but gaining a distinct paunch.

On the website, he'd used an old photo—not that old, only two or three years' old—but one looking more flattering, before the thinning hair and the paunch. He wondered if he should have used a more recent, more truthful, photo? *It's too late now.* Surely everyone used a more flattering photo of themselves?

Earlier, he'd studied himself carefully in the bedroom mirror, as he got ready to catch the bus into the city center. At least there were no grey hairs, but that damned bald patch was so obvious. There was no way he could disguise it. Perhaps if he kept his head upright, maybe she wouldn't see it. He combed what remained of once thick black hair so it looked neat and tidy—not that it mattered, all it took one was one breath of air and his hair would be all over the place again. He considered his clothes. The checked sports jacket—smart, but was it too smart? Would it seem he was trying too hard? Would she think he was a bit of an old fogey? In that case, the pair of jeans were a good touch to set off the jacket. He looked himself up and down, then glanced back at the mirror.

Thing was, aside from those fleeting moments spent gazing in at the restaurant as he walked past, he knew virtually nothing about it, just that it was part of the hotel, and that it was very classy, pretentious and expensive. He picked up a tie and stood before the mirror hesitantly. A tie—was that going too far? He tried it on. No, that was ridiculous. He'd look like her father if he wore that.

The hotel was reputed to be one of the oldest in Cambridge. To one side the medieval university buildings hemmed it in, separated by just a narrow cobbled alleyway. On the other side of the hotel was the busy traffic junction Simon walked past every day on his way to and from the office. It was hard, amid all this bustle, to imagine that a short walk down a few twisty side streets would lead to the huge open space of the common, stretching away into the distance.

He'd gaze in at the hotel restaurant, hardly imagining some day he'd be sitting inside. From outside, through the high windows, he caught glimpses of ornately decorated walls, high chandeliers, and tasteful reproductions of Old Masters. It was the sort of place frequented by tourists, visiting businessmen, and well-off parents treating their university offspring to a good meal.

Uniformed waiters glided between tables as if in slow motion as they poured glasses of champagne or wine, nothing disturbing their calm, methodical air of detachment. Diners and drinkers sometimes met his gaze as they idly stared out of the windows, well removed from the life on the street outside, with its endless herds of passers-by, beggars lying in doorways calling out for spare change, and the perpetually queueing traffic, periodically interrupted by the urgent sirens and blue lights of police cars, ambulances or fire engines speeding past the stopped traffic.

Now Simon was on the other side of the glass and could see the restaurant at first hand. He was now one of those drinkers idly gazing out. The quiet, the peace, from the noise and bustle of the streets outside made the restaurant seem like an island of serenity, yet despite its calm, he felt ill at ease. His nervousness was heightened by the thought that everyone must know exactly what he was doing there: the staff, in their smart uniforms, from the barman over there in the corner standing proudly guarding the bottles of wine, champagne and spirits, to the waiters smoothly gliding back and forth delivering plates and glasses and bottles. And the other diners in the restaurant, they must know too. It was obvious, and it made Simon even more nervous, and he knew it. He looked at his watch again. He was sweating, and he was looking round the room far too often, he knew, but he couldn't help it.

Another drink, that was what he needed to calm his nerves. *No,* he told himself, *no, try to hold on for a bit or you'll be drunk well before she turns up.*

She still hadn't shown up. He couldn't avoid looking at his watch one more time. It was only four minutes past, but already he felt he'd been waiting for an eternity. He hadn't done anything like this before. It was all new to him, that was why he felt so nervous.

His right hand, grasping the empty wine glass, was clammy with sweat. He'd seen her photos, but you couldn't see her face clearly in any of them. It was either out of focus, or turned to one side, or the camera had cropped it off. The face told you a lot but did it really matter? She said she was twenty-nine but you never really knew with this sort of thing. People lied, took a few years off, even a decade, said all sorts of things. After all, he'd taken a few years off his age himself. But she was bound to be younger than him.

Five past. *Is there any wine left?* He took a last sip. These were big glasses. *Wait till she turns up,* he told himself. Then he found he was tapping his fingers on the table. *Stop it,* he told himself.

To distract himself, he took in his surroundings. The restaurant was about half full, but it was already quite noisy. There was a table full of businessmen, sitting there in suits, ties loosened, guffawing away at each other's jokes, and several tables of people he took to be tourists, dressed in T-shirts and shorts, looking in awe at their surroundings. In the far corner, tucked away at a table for two, a couple sat gazing at each other, hardly saying a word. He was the only person sitting on his own.

Seven minutes past. *Is she standing me up? Give it a bit more time*, he thought, *stop panicking*. But he couldn't avoid that feeling that the whole restaurant was staring at him, judging him for what he was. And just what was he? Just a sad middle aged man on a blind date.

He'd looked at her photos on the website, at the whole of her profile, a thousand times, it seemed. Even today, he'd gone online to see it again, just to refresh his memory, even though he could recite by heart her likes and dislikes, and her description of herself. He tried to visualize his favorite photo, out of her six photos on the website. It was the one taken on a sunny day with her face out of focus. Despite the blurring on the photo you could see she had long curly red hair. Her figure was slim, and she was wearing a leather jacket with jeans, leaning up against a brick wall. It might have been from a CD cover, it reminded him of the first Elastica album. Maybe that's what she was, some up and coming star, with the photo off of her latest CD. He laughed to himself realizing how ridiculous that was. Of course, she wasn't even remotely famous, or why would she be on the website? He laughed, and one of the men in suits at the neighboring table looked across, his gaze seeming to take him in for a moment before looking away.

Would she look anything like her photos? What if hers were years out of date too? Someone appeared to one side of him, and he glanced round quickly, thinking it might be her. But it wasn't, it was the waiter.

"Another glass of wine?"

He nodded. There was, after all, no sign of her, and now it was twelve minutes past. The second hand on his watch ticked resolutely on. *She isn't going to turn up, is she?* He was going to be left sitting here all night. Fancy imagining anything else would happen.

Thirteen. The waiter placed another large glass at his elbow. My God, even if she did ever show up, he'd have long since drunk himself into oblivion. His phone buzzed, making him jump. A text message—it could only be her.

"So sorry, I'm running late—but I'll be with you real soon. I am excited to meet you! Rachel X"

Soon. Soon could mean anything, but at least she was going to turn up. It was all going ahead. He took a large gulp of wine to celebrate. All those messages they'd exchanged on the site, and now, at last, they were going to meet.

Night after night, he'd logged on to the site, searching, searching for someone. Sometimes he'd find someone he thought might be nice, but it never worked out. They'd suddenly stop replying, or they'd say they'd met someone. Once or twice he'd got close, but it would never lead anywhere except disappointment. So when he saw Rachel's profile, his finger paused for a long time before pressing the SEND MESSAGE button. He sighed afterward. There was something about her—but he was setting himself up for disappointment. She was bound to be just like the rest. Days went by and gradually he found himself logging on to the site less and less. She'd been his last hope, and now he saw that the site was just a waste of time. But then one night, simply out of idle curiosity, he thought he'd just look to see if there was anything in his inbox. It was about ten days afterward, he'd long since given up hope she'd respond when to his surprise he saw it said: "You have 1 new message". There was a reply—and it was from Rachel!

"Real sorry it's taken me a while to respond," she said. "I've been super busy the past week or so, I've been in Germany."

Immediately, without waiting or thinking, he dashed off a reply. After that, messages flowed thick and fast between them. This was looking promising. On some evenings, replies to his messages would arrive within minutes. He hardly dared to hope, crossing his fingers after sending each one.

"What are you looking for?" she asked him after they'd been exchanging messages for a week or so.

He told her. He'd always known ever since he found the website.

She didn't reply. Long minutes dragged on as he sat at his laptop. Nothing. Had he said the wrong thing, had he offended her? Not on this site, surely. Sometimes that just happened, though, you'd exchange messages, and the other person simply didn't reply at all, and you never heard from them again. She had to be different, though, surely she wasn't like that.

He pressed the refresh button to check for new messages. Nothing. He pressed it over and over again, and still nothing. He must have put her off. It was nearly midnight, and he was about to give up and go to bed for the night, when, to his surprise, up popped a new message.

"That all sounds fine. Should we arrange to meet with each other?"

"Yes," he typed, quickly pressing the button to send in case she changed her mind, thinking yes, yes, yes, of course. He sat there, waiting to see if there would be a reply and within a minute or so a new message flashed up.

"Great. I like to get to know someone over a meal first," she replied. "I hope that's okay with you."

"Of course," he said. "What type of food do you like?"

"I'm a bit persnickety with my tastes. I can suggest a few places we can go."

She listed several restaurants and hotels. The only one he recognized was the hotel in the city center, the one he passed every day.

And now he was here. He kept observing the room as he drank more wine and looked at his watch. Seventeen. The waiting had to be the worst part, didn't it? Nothing to do except drink. It was interminable yet exciting. He tried to imagine what she'd look like in the flesh. Would she be wearing that same leather jacket from the photo? He guessed not. He tried to imagine further, but it was all a blank, he couldn't think what her face would look like. He could see the red curly hair, but nothing more, beyond that it was like a dream where things weren't fully visualized.

His phone buzzed again.

"I'm in a taxi. I'm five minutes away. I will see you very soon! R X".

Eighteen minutes past. So she should be here by twenty-five past past. He took another huge gulp of wine but halfway through swallowing stopped and swilled it round his mouth, trying to slow things down and taste the wine first. *God, half the glass is gone already.* He couldn't carry on drinking at this rate, or he'd be totally plastered. Friends had told him before that now you had to keep your wits about you on a date, especially the first one. It was important not to be sloshed in case you found yourself saying or doing something stupid.

Another text.

"Two minutes," it read. "I'm wearing a black dress and high heels. I can't wait to see you! R X"

Definitely not the leather jacket then. His watch read twenty minutes past.

He never saw her arrive. How had that happened? He'd kept scanning the room, watching the entrance hall intently, but suddenly something made him look up from his glass, and she was standing there. Her face was pretty, framed by the red curls he'd seen in the photo, with pale, freckled skin and animated, large grey eyes with prominent, hooded lids. She looked young, she could even have been in her early twenties, there was something curiously unformed in her. Her skin, almost white, contrasted starkly with the black dress, which started somewhere above her knees, showing pale, bare legs below. He couldn't help staring, hardly believing this young, beautiful creature could be Rachel, his date. Then he realized he was sitting there with his mouth agape.

She stood dead still in front of him, her small mouth forming a half smile, her lips almost blood red as she absently licked them. On one side of her mouth was a small mole.

"Simon?" she said, in an American accent. "Hi."

"Sorry," he said. "You must be Rachel."

She laughed, a soft melodic laugh, like the sound of fingers softly playing on a wine glass.

"Yeah—but you're not sorry that I'm Rachel? You English are always saying sorry."

"No, no—"'

"I'm only teasing."

Quickly he rose to his feet as he realized she was standing above him with a good view of his bald patch. He got up too quickly, not pushing the chair fully back, and knocked the table. With the same, his glass—only a quarter full now—spilled over the pure white of the tablecloth, before rolling to the edge of the table, stopping for an agonizing second, as if unsure what it would do, then smashing onto the tiled floor, shards flying in all directions. Conversation stopped as the other diners looked round. For a moment after the glass breaking, there was complete silence.

"Oh my God," she said, far too loudly, touching his arm, as his face started to get hot. "Are you okay?"

"Just my pride," he said as a waiter rushed up, carrying a dustpan and brush, and began sweeping up the glass on the floor.

"I'm sorry," he said to the waiter. The maitre d' came over and ushered them to another table. The hub-hub of conversation in the restaurant began to slowly recover.

"What a disaster," he said as they sat down. *At least,* he thought, *this table isn't facing a mirror.* Instead, it was close to a window, looking out onto the busy junction. He wondered what people looking in made of them as a couple.

"Not at all," she said. He couldn't place which part of America her accent was from. It would give him something to ask her.

"It's great to meet you," she said, holding out her hand.

"I guess the night's already gone with a bang," he said nervously.

She gave that same quiet laugh.

"Really, it's fine. Are you hurt? Did the glass hit you?"

"No—but what about you?"

"That is so sweet of you! I thought I felt a piece of glass fly past. I stepped on something and it crunched under my foot." As he watched, she took off her left shoe under the table, and he found himself unable not to stare at her tiny, delicate foot, as she wriggled her toes, noticing the nails painted the same vivid red as her lips.

"But I'm fine. I sure don't need the emergency room!"

She replaced the high heel.

"Can I get you something?" he said.

"Wine. I'll have a large glass of Sauvignon Blanc."

"So…"

She reached for his hand.

"You're nervous! That's so cute. I don't bite. That's a joke, by the way."

"You're American then? It didn't say on your profile."

She made that gentle, tinkling laugh again.

"I like to keep certain things a mystery until we meet up with each other."

"Which part of America are you from?"

"I grew up on the East Coast. Washington DC."

"And what are you doing here in England?"

"I'm on a scholarship at the university. I'm doing a Masters in History of Art."

"That's something I know nothing about."

"I could teach you."

"I'd love that."

"Sure. I can tell you all about it."

"All those emails and there's still lots to learn about you."

"I have to be super careful about what I reveal until we meet in person. Also... I don't want my college to find out..."

"I understand. Nothing wrong with being cautious."

She smiled, revealing impossibly white teeth. "And like I said, it's good to keep an element of mystery—if I told you everything beforehand, then we have nothing left to talk about."

"Still, I feel I know you from all those messages."

"Mmm. It's good to build up an impression of the other person, but of course, it's always one dimensional. It's never going to be like meeting up in person."

Only a third of her glass was left. How had she done that, he wondered? She'd been talking, and it hadn't seemed she'd been gulping it down, not like the way he'd been drinking.

"Have you done this before?" she asked.

"No. You?"

"Really? You've never done it before?"

"No. Never. Have you?"

Her smile disappeared for a moment. She wagged her little finger, and a golden bangle on her bare arm jangled.

"You shouldn't ask me that."

He felt an uncomfortable pause before she spoke again. "So I've told you a bit more about me... now, what about you?"

"I'm an accountant."

"There you are... something mysterious about you, you never told me that... are you married?"

He hesitated.

Her eyes were unfathomable, like the calm water of a deep lake, as she studied his face.

"Look, it's okay if you are. It doesn't matter to me. I'm just trying to build up a three-dimensional impression of you."

He swallowed hard. "Divorced."

"How long since—"

"A year."

"Wow, that's tough. How long were you married?"

"Five years."

"Do you need more wine?"

"It definitely helps."

He took a large gulp, felt even more loosened from restraint.

"And do you have children?"

"Two daughters."

"Well, that's sweet."

"I don't see them anymore."

"Oh… I'm so sorry."

She leaned on one elbow and studied him.

"And now you're here."

"I'm sure I'm too old for you." The words came out before he could stop them.

She touched his arm. "Don't worry. Listen, Simon, it's absolutely normal in the context we're in. And you're a sweet guy. I'm not here to judge you, I sure hope you don't judge me either."

"So, Rachel, what brought you here?"

Her mouth pursed and she looked puzzled. "A taxi?"

"No, I mean—"

"Oh, I get it… you mean—"

"Yeah."

"Right."

"If you don't mind telling me, that is."

"So I'm on a scholarship over here, but I've still got living costs. And my parents got wiped out in the Crash, some real bad investments. So I can't rely on them for money. And this sure is an expensive country."

"And you—"

"Shall we order?"

"Yes."

She clicked her fingers nonchalantly towards the waiter. The elderly couple at the table behind looked round, their faces showing dismay. She clicked her fingers a second time, and they looked away. The waiter glided over, a flicker of disapproval on his face.

"Yes, madam?"

"I'll have the steak medium rare, with a side salad, no potatoes—"

"It does come with potatoes," said the waiter, looking around as if pretending he wasn't really there.

"Oh. Can you not just leave the potatoes out?"

She looked at Simon.

"I know…" she threw up her hands, "I'm persnickety, but I figure when you're an adult you can eat what you want."

"You're choosy about what you put in your mouth." He smirked as he said it.

"What? Is that funny? Is it something I said? You English have this strange sense of humor."

"Nothing, it's just—"

"Oh…" she pulled a face. "I see—"

"Sorry. That wasn't really… You know… I've often dreamt of meeting an American girl. Always wanted to." In his embarrassment, he felt words tumbling out of him like boulders down a hillside. She laughed that soft laugh again.

"And now you have. That's so great that you've achieved that dream."

"So… how does, I mean… how do we… how does it work?"

"Like I said, we have a meal and see how we get on and then… you totally haven't done this before, have you?" She smiled.

"I think it's going well,"' she said. "Aside from that thing you said just now…" She shuddered. "But it's fine.."

"I didn't mean to offend—"

"It's just… up till then, you seemed such an English gentleman."

"Sorry."

"It's so cute the way you English always say sorry." She put her knife and fork down. "But it's okay, really."

"Good."

"Well, that's so great. I always like to exchange messages first, but it's totally one-dimensional, you know? You never get a full impression of someone. It's super lacking in depth. That's why it's so great to see you in person. And I think this is really going to work out."

"I'm so pleased you think so."

"Sure."

"I like your dress."

"That's very sweet of you. You're very English you know."

He felt himself blush, but couldn't avoid watching her delicate, careful movements as she cut the steak up, at odds with the sheer speed with which she shoveled the meat into her mouth, and drained the wine glass.

"What did your parents do?"

"This is like a job interview."

She looked puzzled for a moment. Her lip quivered minutely.

"So. It's very important we both get some background on each other. After all—"

She reached for his hand. "You seem nice, Simon."

"So do you. This is just so romantic. I'm glad we met."

"'You know what? Me too. I've been so excited."

"I'm enjoying this evening."

"Well, that's super. I feel it's gone really well too."

Her eyes were large and luminous as he looked across the table at her. The small mole on her face had been distracting him all through dinner; he hadn't been able to stop staring at it; as she ate, the mole kept moving to and fro.

"I'm happy to…" she hesitated, licking her lips, "proceed further if you are."

"I think so too."

"You think so? Are you not sure?"

"Yes, yes, I mean, let's. I'm very sure."

"That's great.. Then we just need to sort out the formalities."

"Formalities?"

Before answering, she turned, putting her hand out to stop a passing waiter.

"Hey, could I get more wine?" she demanded. "My glass is totally empty."

Leaning back towards Simon, she hissed, "My fee. The money. I thought a thousand every month."

Five Dates in Room 405

Kara Dennison

The old woman turned and smiled. "And who might this be from?"

"Gent over at the table by the kitchen, ma'am," the waiter replied, nodding to the glass of wine in her hand. "He said to tell you if you like it, the bottle is over with him and you're welcome to more."

"Well, isn't he clever?" She glanced over at the man in question, doing her best to keep from looking as though she was, well, looking. "Thank you, sir."

The waiter nodded and slipped away into the low hum of the hotel restaurant. The woman looked down at the glass, swirling the wine around in it.

I can't drink this.

Then she saw her reflection in the glass and rolled her eyes. *Stupid. Of course, you can.* And she took a large swallow of the red wine.

She nearly coughed it right back up, but aware that there were eyes on her, she blinked back the sudden tears that sprang to her eyes and kept her expression steady, swallowing the mouthful of wine. It burned far more than she'd expected it to. Everyone acted like wine was something sweet and smooth… she'd expected it to be more like chocolate. But this was… old fruit juice.

That's literally what wine is, Carrie.

She sniffed, glanced around to see if she'd attracted attention, and seeing she hadn't, took a more casual sip this time. It was better in small amounts, less intense. Still with a strange tingling burn to it that she couldn't register as pleasant, but not terrible.

She glanced over at the man. He was in his sixties, perhaps, but carrying it surprisingly well. Still, he was… *in his sixties.*

"So are you," she said under her breath, glaring at her reflection again. And, cradling the bulb of the wine glass in one palm, she walked toward the table.

★★★★

"I can't believe you actually said yes to Chad."

Carrie sat still on the edge of the hotel bed, wincing as Maria brushed out her tangle of hair. "Well, no one else asked me."

"He's the last guy in the school anyone would go with."

"And I'm the last girl in the school anyone would go with."

Maria made an odd grumbling noise under her breath, like a pot about to boil over. "But then if the last guy and the last girl get together, you're the most embarrassing couple. Get it?"

"Yeah, but it's either that or not go… and going to prom is what you do."

"No." Maria tapped Carrie gently on top of the head with the hairbrush. "You could've come alone."

"Dateless?"

"Too cool for a date."

Carrie ran her tongue over her braces. "That's not the way people would have seen it… Geez, ow! Come on!"

"If you used conditioner, this wouldn't be happening."

"Conditioner's expensive." Carrie braced herself on the bed, looking down at the seam of the pantyhose stretched across her toes. "Seriously, it was either this or stay home, and I don't want to be the girl who stayed home from prom. Even if that means going with Chad Masterson."

Maria climbed off the bed. "I'm gonna get some detangler. Hang tight."

Carrie hung tight.

All things considered, there was nothing wrong with Chad. He'd sit in the back of AP calculus programming games into everyone's graphing calculators, after all. He was smart and awkward, and he wasn't *unattractive*. Hell, there were popular boys who were unattractive inside and out, and the girls were kicking each other in the face for a chance to take them to prom. Maria included.

Carrie hadn't even felt bad about going with Chad until Maria told her she ought to feel bad. And now, there was this feeling of dissatisfaction, this concern that they really were just the last two losers on the playground, and that everyone would see them that way and laugh as soon as they walked in. Even her dress—which was damned beautiful, honestly, a sort of teal thing with drop shoulders and a bodice that belonged on a Disney princess—didn't make her feel any less of a sore thumb in all this.

"Could you go without your glasses?" Maria asked as she came back from the hotel room's little bathroom, a bottle of detangler in her hair.

"No, I couldn't go without my glasses."

Maria sighed and leaned in, plucking the glasses from Carrie's face by the bridge. "Hmm. Yeah. That looks good, actually."

"I can't see now. You're just a big brown and white blur."

"That makes it better, then. You won't have to see anyone or anything." She tossed the glasses into Carrie's lap. "Including Chad."

"He's fine. God. Why so much hate for him?"

"I don't hate him. I just…" She shrugged, climbing back onto the bed and spritzing the detangler in Carrie's hair. "You could do better."

"No, I couldn't."

"Don't shake your head. Hold still."

Carrie fell silent, allowing Maria to tug and twist and wrench her hair up into something that was allegedly nice. Maria jabbed a few hairpins and barrettes in place, and Carrie's scalp screamed with pain as several strands of her hair were tugged within an inch of being ripped out.

"Ow," she muttered.

Maria patted Carrie's shoulder as she got back off the bed in search of hairspray. "You'll stop feeling it in a minute. That's the only way to get it to stay. One sec."

"I just wish you'd stop acting like you're protecting me against some sort of social disaster," Carrie muttered quietly.

"Well?" Maria shook up the hairspray bottle. "It's prom night? Your name *is* Carrie? I'm not taking any chances."

Carrie grimaced. "Wow, that's totally the first time I've heard that one."

"I'm kidding." Maria began spritzing the chemically floral spray around Carrie's head. "Mostly. Seriously, though, I just want you to have a nice time."

"And that's why you're telling me that everyone's gonna judge my date and my hair and my glasses?"

Maria stepped back, tapping the bottom of the hairspray bottle against one palm. Carrie couldn't tell whether Maria was appreciating her handiwork or weighing her words. Potentially both.

"Having a nice time doesn't always mean having a good time. Not in high school." She put the hairspray down next to the room's flat-screen TV. "I'm gonna go put on my makeup. Just hang out for a bit, and I'll come back and do yours."

"Fine."

The bathroom door slammed behind Maria. Carrie sighed, looking at her reflection in the dark TV screen opposite the bed. As far as she was concerned, she was plain. Ordinary. And honestly, all things considered, just wanted to be at home in bed with a book and her cat. It was just… proms were what you did, weren't they? And she'd already skipped homecoming, opted out of any spirit week activities that would have involved calling attention to herself… she couldn't just keep not doing high school things. She couldn't stand the idea of graduating without having done any of the things she was meant to do.

Though why she was 'meant' to do them, she wasn't sure.

"Who makes those rules?" she muttered, lying back on the bed. She winced and sat up immediately when one of the tightly-placed hairpins jabbed her scalp. "Ugh…"

Honestly—and she'd never tell Maria, and she really wouldn't tell Chad—the only reason she hadn't just faked sick was because she didn't want Chad to think she was canceling on his account. Like Maria had said, he was not particularly popular. She had nothing against him, and she knew how she'd feel if someone ducked out on her on a night like this.

Relieved? a little voice in the back of her mind asked.

She laughed. *Maybe.* But she wasn't sure. She didn't want to take that chance and inadvertently ruin someone else's evening. Besides, her mom had dropped plenty of 'subtle' hints—if she didn't start at least keeping an eye out for someone now, she wouldn't be ready for the dating scene when the right one did come along.

"I only have so many chances." Carrie stared at her shoes. "Especially someone like me. For all I know, this'll be the only date I ever go on. I shouldn't just duck out. Should I?"

The TV switched on.

"Ugh, Maria, I don't want the extra noise right now…" But when Carrie looked up, she saw that the remote was resting next to the television on the dresser, by a glass of water she had poured for herself but not gotten to. It had switched on by itself. And judging by the gentle shuffling around in the bathroom, Maria hadn't heard anything out of the ordinary.

Carrie looked at the TV. It wasn't any show she knew… honestly, it didn't seem like a show at all. It was more like a first-person view of a random backyard; nothing particularly cinematic about it. She got up, walking toward the TV to get a closer look without putting on her glasses.

"Hey, Carrie, where are you going?"

"Oh, I was just looking at—"

Carrie turned around and gasped.

She wasn't in the hotel room anymore. Rather, she appeared to be in the backyard she'd seen on the TV. She was looking right at three strangers—two boys and a girl, all college-aged or thereabouts—sitting in lawn chairs and wearing summer clothes. There was an empty chair next to them with a cell phone on it—much smaller and sleeker than hers, but with her capybara charm hanging from it even so.

"Just… what?" one of the boys asked.

"No, uh…" Carrie looked down at herself. She was barefoot, wearing cutoff shorts and a tank top. She could see that clearly. She put a hand to her face… no glasses.

"You okay, Care-Bear?" the girl asked.

Carrie flinched at the childhood nickname. "Don't call me that."

The girl looked surprised. "Sorry, I… you said you didn't mind."

Carrie blinked. "Did… I?"

"Finals," the boy who'd spoken before said. He waved a hand to Carrie. "Come on over here. Lie down. Relax. I told you, you were studying too much. Time to chill."

Still confused, Carrie walked over to the group, lying down on the vacant lawn chair. The other three went back to looking up at the sky.

"I thought they were supposed to have started like ten minutes ago," said the boy who hadn't spoken yet. He was next to Carrie, shirtless and stretched out on his chair. And cute, Carrie couldn't help but notice. She felt herself blush.

"Eh, they're always late." The girl shrugged, pulling her knees up to her chin. "Besides, I think there were budget cuts this year, so they can't do the big light show like they did for Blowout last year. Right on our year, too, huh?" She looked over at Carrie and laughed; Carrie got the impression that they were friends and laughed back.

"Heh. Yeah. Just our luck."

The other girl rolled her eyes. "Greg, check her temperature."

The boy next to her rolled over onto his side, putting a hand on her forehead. She blushed even more. "Well, she's heating up now…"

"Stop it," she hissed, embarrassed.

"But she's fine." He smiled gently, and she felt her heart melt. "Like you said. Just too much studying."

"Honestly Car…C-Carrie…" The girl stuttered away from the nickname. Carrie felt guilty. Wherever she was, whoever this was, apparently she'd given her permission to use it for some reason.

"It's fine," she said, waving her hand dismissively. "I just got… uh… grumpy."

The girl smiled. "Oh, I know. I know you well enough for that. Anyway. We're gone after finals. You're doing amazing in every class, last I checked.

Relax. There's pretty much no way you can fail any of your classes, right?"

"Uh…"

Greg patted Carrie on the shoulder. "Nah, the Thomas Hardy seminar is pretty rough. Didn't you say your final is like half your grade?"

"Y-Yeah," Carrie stammered.

"Geez." The girl reached for a bottle and handed it over to Carrie. "Lighten up. Relax. That's what we're here for."

Carrie glanced at the bottle. Beer. "N-No thanks."

The girl blinked. "But this is your favorite."

"I… I'm just not feeling it tonight."

Greg got to his feet, offering Carrie a hand. "Come on. Let's take a walk."

For some reason, she felt far more comfortable with this stranger than the other strangers. She took his hand and let herself be led to a brick walkway lined with street lamps.

This was a college campus, no doubt about it. The peculiarly 'Old Academic' aesthetic, absolutely everything made of brick, tended lawns and brand new fixtures made in 19th-century style… only colleges and city centers ever looked like that.

"Hey." Greg put an arm around her shoulder. She didn't flinch, it seemed like an easy motion, meant to comfort rather than to invade. Did she know him, too? "Did you and Jess have a fight or something?"

That was the problem; she didn't know. "N-No?" she guessed. "I don't… think so."

"You just seem really confused. I mean, I know stress wears you out, but this is more than usual."

Carrie looked up at Greg. His eyes were soft with concern.

"Honestly?" She looked around herself. "I'm... I... five minutes ago I was in a hotel room with my friend Maria doing my hair before prom, and now suddenly it's apparently my senior year of college, and I'm..."

Greg laughed. "You, too, huh?"

"What?"

"I get that sometimes. I'll just be walking down the street, not thinking about anything, and suddenly I'm just like... 'Oh my God, I'm a college senior. I'm allowed to drink. I've gotta find a job.' When I swear like yesterday I was in high school."

"No, that's not what I meant—"

"It's weird, I know." Greg squeezed her shoulder. "But it's okay to feel weird. And, like, I know you've had a hard time what with worrying about jobs when you graduate and whatever... but I honestly think you're going to do fine. Seriously."

Carrie forced a smile. "Thank you... that's nice to hear."

"Hey..." Greg took a deep breath, about to speak. Then he let it out, seeming to change his mind. "Uh..."

"What?"

"Look, I... I know I said the President's Ball was a 'just friends' thing and all, but... Carrie, I had a really great time with you. And I know we're all going our separate ways soon, but I just wanted to say before that, that I..."

Carrie looked up at Greg. "Yes?"

"I... I really do like you. And I'm sorry, I know you told me you just wanted to keep it strictly friends, and I respect that. But I just want you to know that I do like you that much. And that if you ever did… want to…"

Carrie suddenly found herself wishing she had this chunk of memories she was going without—someone who liked her? Someone who didn't think she was an embarrassment to be around? Someone who was nice? Who worried about her? Who respected her after she'd (apparently) said she didn't want a relationship?

"Well… thank you." She felt herself smiling. "Thank you for saying so. That… that really makes me happy."

★★★★

"What makes you happy?"

"Huh?"

Carrie looked over her shoulder, fumbling her glasses out of her lap and onto her face. Maria was standing in the bathroom doorway, one eye perfectly shadowed and lined and blended, the other half done.

"What makes you happy?"

"Oh, I… I think that was the TV…" She glanced over, but the television had rather unhelpfully turned itself off.

Maria rolled her eyes. "Almost done." She turned and went back into the bathroom. Carrie watched her leave, baffled.

What did I just see? It had seemed extremely real. Unquestionably. And she'd never been one for daydreams, realistic or otherwise. She really had been there. Wherever "there" was. The future. Some other life. And for just a few minutes, she hadn't been the least likable person in the group. By all accounts, she'd turned someone else down.

Was that her future?

She snickered. *Not likely.*

The TV turned on again, almost as soon as she'd had the thought. Carrie raised her head to look. Now she could see what looked like some sort of resort, decked out in white and gold decorations. There were people in suits and dresses milling around.

"Nah," she said in a low whisper, closing her eyes, "I'm not ready for another flash forward."

"Oh, I know how you feel," said an unfamiliar voice.

Carrie opened her eyes with a start. She was at the resort now, sitting next to an older woman in a teal skirt suit. "I never thought I'd see the day, personally." She paused awkwardly. "Oh, I know that sounds terrible of me, but… you know what I mean."

No, I don't. "Y-Yeah."

"But it's lovely, isn't it?" The woman smiled, she bore a bit of a resemblance to Carrie's Auntie Kate, but a bit narrower around the jawline, a few more years down the line. "It was such a beautiful wedding."

"Ah. Yes, it was." Carrie looked out the window onto what looked like a golf course. "Heh. Um. So… silly question, but… who got married?"

The woman who looked so much like Auntie Kate—who, Carrie suddenly thought, probably was Auntie Kate—stared for a moment, then burst out laughing. "Oh, Care, you had such a straight face, I thought you were serious!"

It was then that Carrie happened to glance down at herself… in her white wedding dress.

My wedding day?

She looked around quickly. So she ended up marrying Greg after all?

"Where is he?" she asked, mostly to herself.

"Oh, Chris? He was just in the restroom." Aunt Kate chuckled. "He'll be out in a minute, and then you can go on to the reception." And with a gentle pat on Carrie's bare shoulder, she was off.

"… Chris?"

Carrie stared down at her hand, confused. A glittering engagement ring and a thin gold band set on top of it. She felt strangely lightheaded, strangely warm. She'd never considered marriage seriously, largely because it seemed so big and permanent. You did a huge ceremony, you pledged yourself to another human being until one of you died, and then you moved all your stuff in with them into a house, and you were together.

Something about it terrified her. But here she was.

"There's my Care-Bear…"

Carrie looked in the direction of the voice. It wasn't Greg. It wasn't anyone she recognized. He was about her height, darker complexioned and with prominent features that classed him as cute—maybe even 'comical'—more than handsome. But he exuded charm and calm and affection somehow.

Apparently, she trusted him enough to let him use the nickname she hated.

"Hey, you." Her voice sounded small and wobbly in her own ears. *Chris. Auntie Kate said his name is Chris.* She at least had an advantage there where she hadn't before. "Chris." And she smiled awkwardly.

Chris laughed, taking Carrie by the hand. "Oh, good, you remember me. Thought I'd lost my shot as soon as I was out of sight."

"N-No. Heh." She laughed it off, seeing that he was doing the same. She wasn't ready to go so far as to say she could see why she married him… but she could see why she'd enjoyed his company, at least.

"Well? You ready for the reception?" He offered his arm with an extra dose of old-fashioned romantic flair. Carrie found herself taking it as if it were the most natural thing in the world, and the two walked together to the hall where the reception would be held.

"I'm… not sure," Carrie said honestly. "I… I still can't believe I'm married, honestly."

"Yeah." Chris exhaled over a laugh. "It's kind of made out to be a big deal, isn't it?"

Carrie peered at him curiously as they walked. "Well, it is kind of a big deal, last I checked."

"I mean, yeah, but… It's you and me. You know? Just us. Together like we have been for three years now. And yet they walk us up an aisle to talk to a guy in a dress like we're being led to sacrifice or something. When, you know, what's gonna change? A tax break and no one asking whether or not we're using protection."

"A… aha." Carried blushed.

Chris gave her a gentle nudge and leaned over to give her a peck on the cheek. "It doesn't matter how it happened, though. I'm just glad it did."

"Y-Yeah… me, too." She looked up at Chris. He seemed to be telling the truth. Normally whenever a guy said anything even remotely affectionate to her, it was revealed to be a joke mere seconds later. But he seemed really earnest about it. Really, really in love.

She looked away.

"Thank you," she said quietly.

★★★★

"Yeah, you better thank me."

Carrie's head snapped up. Maria was standing in front of her again, her fists full of brushes and makeup containers. "You're so flinchy when I do your makeup, this is a big sacrifice on my part."

She was back. No Chris. No wedding. No reception. Just her and her prom dress and her uncomfortable hairdo. She stuttered to herself as Maria dumped the makeup on the bed, picking out a little white tube.

"B–But… how is this…"

"Shh. Take off your glasses and look at me."

Carrie turned her face forward obediently, removing her glasses. Maria began smoothing some sort of cool cream over her face. "What's that?" Carrie asked.

"Primer."

"Like for cars?"

"Like for… no, it's so your makeup looks right. 'Like for cars.' Sheesh."

Carrie fell silent and let Maria dab away at her face with sponges and brushes and fingers. That peculiarly antique smell to the powder, the thick chemical smell of the lipstick that reminded her of late winter evenings preparing for her bit parts in school plays. She closed her eyes, letting her mind wander.

★★★★

"You alone?" a man's voice asked.

The smell of lipstick and powder gave way to the smell of salt and suntan lotion. Oh, what now… Carrie opened her eyes tentatively.

It was a beach. No, not just *a* beach… the one near her house. The dry chill of the hotel room had given way to a humid heat. She was sitting in a beach chair, bare feet sporting manicured toenails. The man standing over her wasn't Greg or Chris… he was in his forties, perhaps, in a polo shirt and khaki shorts. Not bad looking.

"I…" She looked around, then back up at the man. "This is going to sound strange, but I'm honestly not sure."

He cracked a smile. "Not surprised. I imagine you get a lot of attention."

Carrie put a hand to her face to hide the blush she was sure was forming. When she did, she noticed the rings—engagement and wedding—a bit age-worn, but still there as they had been at her wedding.

The man noticed, too. "Ah. Subtle. Point taken."

"I… what?" She looked at her hand. "Oh, you thought I was showing you…"

"No, no…" He put his hands up, offering her a forced smile that seemed more upset than apologetic. "I can take a hint. Seriously."

She hadn't been offering a hint… but all things considered, it was probably better she'd done so inadvertently. "Was there… something you needed?"

"No… ah, well…" He leaned down conspiratorially. "It's probably not wise for your husband to leave you all alone on a beach like this is all I'll say."

Carrie bristled. "I'm not a puppy. Last I checked, I can look after myself."

The man reared away, suddenly looking offended. "That's no way to take a compliment."

"What compliment? You just basically said I'm up for grabs unless my husband is hovering over me. What's complimentary about that?"

"That's not what I said."

"It literally is." Carrie spotted a book lying next to her on a towel and picked it up. Wuthering Heights, well worn. She remembered having read it three times by her senior year. How many times had she read it now? "Now excuse me. Important reading to do."

The man narrowed his eyes at her. "I'd hate to see how you treat your husband."

Carrie sniffed, opening to the bookmark. "Exactly as well as he treats me." She glanced up at him. "Same as you. Good-bye."

"You coulda had me, you know."

"Why would I want you?" She flashed her rings again.

The man opened his mouth, closed it, muttered a few choice words under his breath, and stalked off. Carrie snickered.

★★★★

"Hold still, dammit."

"Huh?" Carrie's eyes snapped open. Maria was nose-to-nose with her, a mascara wand in her hand.

Again…

"Whatever's so funny, forget it for a sec. I can't do your makeup if you're bopping around giggling over things."

Carrie held still obediently. She still seethed a bit at the man—why, though, she wasn't sure. He hadn't been real. Well, not yet.

Yet?

"Maria?"

"Hmm."

"Have you ever, like, had your life flash before your eyes?"

Maria tilted Carrie's head back with one hand for a better view of her face. "Yeah. The time my dad caught Janine Murray and me making out in his computer room."

"You and…" *Huh.* "I mean… no, I mean like… have you ever seen your future?"

"Nnnnope. Can't say that I have. I'd kill to, though. How cool would that be?"

"Yeah, heh." Carrie paused. "So, uh, if it ever did happen to you, what would you think was—"

"Shh. Lipstick time."

Carrie silenced herself as Maria applied liner, then some sort of liquid lipstick, then blotted and applied again.

"And there you go. You're ready." She glanced at Carrie's phone. "Go ahead and text Chad that you'll be down in a minute. I'm gonna go on."

"Sure."

"Unless you want me to wait with you?"

"N-No." Carrie shook her head. "I'm good."

Maria shrugged. "Suit yourself."

Carrie wiggled a bit where she sat. "How do I look?"

"Fine."

"Just 'fine'?"

Maria smiled helplessly. "Cut it out. I'll see you downstairs."

That wasn't the answer I was hoping for, Carrie thought bitterly. She reached for her phone and texted Chad, squinting myopically at her phone's screen.

"All done. In room 405. See you in ten?"

She set the phone aside and glanced back at the TV. "Got anything else for me before I go?" she muttered. Though the third instance hadn't involved the TV at all. Which meant there was something else going on. What it was… she wasn't entirely sure. Nor was she entirely sure how she felt about it.

A college friend with a crush. A guy who seemed perfectly happy to get married to her. A guy who apparently found her attractive until she was taken… and none of them were Chad. None of them were high school boys.

She reached for the water glass on the end table—

And found herself reaching for a glass of wine.

"I… didn't ask for this," she blurted out.

"It's a gift," said a waiter at her shoulder…

Cradling the bulb of the wine glass in one palm, she walked toward the table.

"I hear this is from you," Carrie said, sitting in the chair the man pushed out for her.

"You seemed very lonely on your own." He sounded kind, with a touch of an accent. *British? Scottish?*

Carrie glanced covertly at her own left hand. No rings, and no sign that rings had been removed recently. Chris… had they divorced? Had he died?

"Who was he?" the man asked, glancing at something hanging around her neck.

She looked down. The wedding ring. *Oh.*

"He… he was…" Carrie pursed her lips, turning the ring over between her fingers. "He was funny. And romantic. And very sweet. And I feel like I only knew him for a few seconds."

"It's never long enough, is it?"

Carrie smiled. "It seems like nothing ever is."

The man sipped at his own glass of wine. "Lost my Sophie six months ago. She was a firecracker." He chuckled. "Met her when I was twenty-one. We got married straight out of college. She just made it to our fortieth."

"I'm so sorry."

"No reason to be sorry for a long and happy life." The man smiled. "Has anyone ever told you you're a very lovely woman?"

Carrie shook her head. "My friend Maria told me I was 'fine' before prom, but that's about it."

"Fah. You deserve far more than 'fine,' my dear."

"That's sweet of you to say."

"I call them as I see them."

Carrie stared at her own wine. "Did anyone ever tell you… you know, when you were young… that if you didn't find someone by high school or college, you never would?"

"Oh, all the time."

"And?"

The man raised the glass to his lips. "Bollocks."

Carrie giggled.

"Ah." The man swallowed. "Maybe you will. Maybe you won't. Maybe you'll find someone when you're thirty. Forty." He glanced at Carrie with a faint smile. "Sixty."

Carrie smiled back.

"Maybe you won't find anyone. And maybe you'll be fine. My sister, she's seventy-two this year, never married. Happy as can be as an aunt. Never needed anyone. Just herself. Well, we're not all so lucky, but it goes to show."

"Mm. I guess it does." She looked over at the man. "You're very sweet. And… really very good-looking. But… I have somewhere to be."

The man nodded. "Go. Maybe I'll see you again after."

"Maybe so."

She got up quickly and walked out of the hotel restaurant—

—right to the door of her hotel room. She opened it. Chad stood waiting, wearing an ill-fitting rented suit and smelling of what was probably his older brother's cologne.

"H-Hey…" Chad waved awkwardly, as though they were standing across the room from each other rather than practically toe to toe. "You, uh… you look… you look nice."

"Well, that's better than Maria gave me."

Chad laughed but stopped himself. "Sorry, was that not funny?"

"No, it's… you're fine." Carrie exhaled and smiled.

"So, uh…" Chad gestured toward the hall. "Are you…"

Carrie frowned. "You don't want to go to the prom, do you?"

"What? No, I-"

"Look." Carrie waved a hand. "We both feel really weird about this. And… and you're nice and stuff. And I wouldn't mind maybe seeing you more after I get to know you as a friend… but is this really 'us'?"

Chad shrugged. "I mean… you go to prom. It's what you do. Right?"

Carrie started unpinning her hair. "There's an arcade right around the corner that's got the new Super Drift G machine in. Would you rather slow-dance in front of a bunch of people who don't even like us, or race me?"

Chad's eyes were wide. "You mean the actual one? Not the American knock-off?"

"No, it's not Drift Machine. I mean it's the actual Japanese one with the little tickets you swipe and the Eurobeat music and everything."

"Holy…" Chad looked down at both their outfits. "But… prom…"

Carrie shrugged. "Something tells me this isn't our only chance at dating. Each other or other people." She kicked off her shoes and went back to the bed to grab her glasses. "So? Prom formal gaming night?"

Chad blinked. Thought. Then grinned. "Yeah. Prom formal gaming night."

Carrie slipped on her sneakers, shook out her hair, and waved Chad toward the door to the stairs. He followed, laughing.

There would be a million opportunities for first dates.

There would be a million opportunities for love.

But there would never be another opportunity to spend prom night playing racing games in a formal dress.

John Loves Alice/ Alice Loves John

Rebecca Redshaw

Alice looked nervously at the crystal clock ticking softly on the vanity. Twelve fifteen. Turning to the large circular mirror, she leaned forward ever so slightly to better focus on the image reflecting back. "One of the blessings of old age," she thought, "is that one's eyesight fades in a timely fashion to the appearance of one's wrinkles."

Reaching out to her reflection she felt the thin layer of dust on her fingertips. "There was a time this would have upset me terribly." Alice shook her head. She sighed and continued to brush her fine hair gently off her forehead. "But that was then."

The phone call had startled her that afternoon last week. Marybeth always called at three o'clock to see if she needed anything from the store for dinner. Alice suspected it was her daughter's attempt at lessening the guilt she had about not visiting more often. This way if Alice did ask her to pick-up a loaf of bread or some teabags, Marybeth could rush in and drop the items, always with the excuse that "Mark and the kids were waiting on dinner," and then be on her way. But the phone had rung at two o'clock.

Alice reached for the violet crystal perfume bottle and gently applied a drop to her index finger then behind each ear closing her eyes as she smelled the at first strong, then drifting fragrance she had worn since her youth.

She knew she was partly to blame for her only child's distance. When Bill died, Alice clung to her daughter and grandchildren in fear of losing everything. Her anger, she recognized now, had been not only at Bill's abandoning her but her jealousy of Marybeth. Her daughter had been given every advantage that Alice never knew growing up, and even though she knew it was wasted energy, Alice couldn't let go of her feelings.

But the phone had rung at two o'clock, not three that afternoon, and when she picked up the receiver on the fourth ring, she felt her heart literally skip a beat when she heard his voice.

"Alice MacKenzie, is that you?"

Touching her hand to her chest, she lowered herself to the needlepoint cushion in the stairwell. It was like she had heard his voice yesterday.

"Alice?" he repeated, "It's John. John Barber."

Clearing her throat ever so slightly she spoke into the receiver, "Yes, John, it's Alice. But it's not MacKenzie anymore, hasn't been for... I can't remember that long ago."

She heard him laugh and again felt the flutter.

"Alice, I don't mean to intrude on your life. It has been almost sixty years, but I came north to go to my grandson's wedding and well, I, I know this may sound silly, but I wonder if you're free, if you would have lunch with me next week?"

She had closed her eyes as he was speaking in his familiar, deliberate pace. Even as a young man, John had always spoken with assurance and steadiness, belying any nervousness either in a classroom debate or on a first date. That's what they had been so many years ago, one another's first date.

The overcast morning was giving way to white clouds with hints of blue peeking around the edges as Alice stood back from the vanity admiring her pink flowered dress. She heard the chime clock on the dining room mantle downstairs strike the half hour. Twelve-thirty.

When Shirley, her best friend and walking partner, called yesterday and asked her to go to the mall, Alice had made up an excuse so lame, she could hardly believe it herself.

"You're getting a pedicure? How peculiar, Alice, what's gotten into you?"

"Oh, it's not my idea. Marybeth and the children have run out of birthday gifts. They gave it to me some time ago, I just thought, oh, why not?"

"Well, you must tell me everything about it and show me those red painted toenails," Shirley laughed into the phone. "I suppose next you'll be going for a mud bath or some wrap kind of thing."

Alice knew once the pedicure lie rolled off her tongue there was no way she could not paint her toenails because surely Shirley would want to see the finished product.

Adjusting her sash Alice fumbled with the small safety pin she attached to the bodice of the dress. No, it was no wonder she didn't tell Shirley or for that matter Marybeth. She could imagine the inflection of her daughter's voice.

"Mother, don't you think it's rather silly to rendezvous at your age?" It was no matter to her daughter that it was only lunch. "I mean it hasn't been that long since Daddy…"

"Oh, my. Oh my," thought Alice as she caught her breath after coming down the stairs.

This way if for some reason John didn't show up, or it was a disastrous lunch she wouldn't have to relive every detail with Shirley, or Marybeth, or anyone. Whatever happened today would be her memory and hers alone.

Reaching for a glass in the cabinet above the kitchen sink, Alice noticed the crookedness of her fingers. She had played the piano for John on that first date and remembered as if it were yesterday the look on his face when she finished the Chopin étude. She seldom played for anyone being too shy and too self-conscious, but he made her feel at ease in the parlor that day and her now arthritic fingers which could barely grasp an empty water glass, had graced the ivory keys like magic.

"Play for me always, Alice." His head rested against the back of the Queen Ann's chair. When she released the sustaining pedal and looked up from the keyboard, she noticed his eyes were closed, and a faint smile crossed his lips. She giggled, as young girls of sixteen do, and he opened his eyes and laughed with her.

"I think you might tire of Frederic Chopin at some point."

"No. Never. And there's always Mozart and Rachmaninoff," he said. "Say, how about Gershwin or Berlin? Can you play one of them?"

The afternoon raced by with each turn of the page. He even sang along. "What'll I do when you are far away…" His soft tenor sang Irving Berlin's lyrics with such clarity she shivered slightly when he leaned over her right shoulder to read the words.

She sipped the lukewarm water slowly trying to calm her nerves and moisten her dry throat.

So many years. More than a lifetime it seemed, and yet they spoke very little on the phone last week. It was almost as if they knew if they talked too much or shared too much of the past, there may not be any need to meet for lunch and she wanted more than anything to see him again.

"Now, no tears," Alice spoke out loud to command herself not to cry. "This is a perfectly pleasant occasion. Lunch with an old friend in town for the day."

The door bell rang. Alice stiffened setting the glass down deliberately, she smoothed her skirt as she stepped toward the entrance way.

Life had been good to her more than not. She'd had forty years of marriage to Bill who was a devoted husband. She had a daughter who at the least gave her two beautiful grandsons and did call once a day.

Looking back at the times one remembers as important, Alice counted more good moments than bad.

But today, for the first time in years and years she felt fresh. John, with just a phone call, had brought a young girl's memories down from the attic, dusted them off with the sound of his voice, and let her remember the magic.

The clock chimed one as she opened the door.

Mismatch.com

Melanie Reitzel

Dear Mr. Ph.D. in Business:

Ronald, I'm sorry I was five minutes late, and we couldn't get a seat at the bar for Happy Hour, so we had to pay full price for the calamari. Next time, to figure out the minimum tip, just double the tax.

Dear Norton:

Twenty-nine guitars?! Wow. And you can really introduce me to Willie Nelson?

Dear Matt:

Uhhhh, do you always try to kiss like that within ten minutes of meeting someone? Sure, I'll come to dinner—as long as your mother chaperones.

Dear Joseph:

Perhaps if you'd told me before the curtain rose that the program belonged on the floor, that the binocular strap was not allowed to hang around my neck, that the handkerchief had to come out of my purse before the curtain went up—and of course I know better than to talk during a performance—I had a grandmother, duh. I know you've dumped women for less than breaking Joseph's Ballet Attendance Rules. I've dumped men for less than having them.

Dear Superman:
I understand your reluctance to post your photo on the dating site—thanks for sending one along. You don't need a cape, blue tights or the insignia on the chest. The grin alone would stop a train.

Dear Brent:
You know if we meet for coffee, I'm not sure I can promise to be wearing the exact shade of lipstick that I am wearing in my profile picture. Oh, wait? Can you hear that? Those are bells going off in my head telling me my afternoon might be better spent cross-filing my knee-highs.

Dear Mike:
4:30 works for me. Which Starbucks? The one on the corner or the one down the street? Let me guess: you'll be dressed in black. Italian loafers, no socks.

Dear Roland:
The picture is recent. And yes, you weigh more than I do. All my teeth (except for two crowns) are my own, and my hair color is natural. No tattoos unless you count the ink on my fingers from if I miss with the eyeliner. My ears are pierced nothing else.
I don't understand your fear of dating someone on anti-depressants, however. Sometimes the brain stops making enough neurotransmitters—just like the pancreas sometimes stops making enough insulin.

Dear Dave:

It's been a hell of a week. When you're back in town, do you suppose we could get ourselves locked in the Miramar Bar again? I'm sorry we yelled for help.

Dear Matt:

I think it's just so damned selfless and self-sacrificing of you to be thinking of my welfare like this—are you sure you're not Catholic? Yours is such a wonderfully male approach to a problem: it's direct, it's focused, it's action centered. It's so: "I have the solution to all your problems right here in my pants."

Dear Universe:

Stop sending me fish. The profile states quite clearly: No Pisces.

Dear Spencer:

Thanks for the latte. Don't worry about being late; I remember parenting teens. I enjoyed our conversation, but I have to say, you talked more like a widower on the lookout for a nanny than a date. Next time you dress for a date, I suggest you draw more attention to your eyes—Dude, wear blue. And really, it's okay you gave your wife's shoes away. Dolce and Gabbana or not, it wouldn't have seemed right to sell them.

Dear Frank:

Oh, you sweetheart, you totally crack me up. Yes, I re-wrote my profile. I think you should read the latest New Yorker first, and then get around to my revisions.

Dear Adam:

Give it up. I'll never be a Republican. And now I don't even want to date one.

Dear Dan:

I appreciate the fact that you keep an open mind about such things as age and appearance, and I'm flattered by your proposal, but I've done a little math—your mother could have been my dorm mate in college. Think of it this way: you self-medicate with beer; I take estrogen.

So, Nature Boy—

How was the body-paint, black-light sixties-retro nude dance at your "special club?"

Dear RevEmUp:

How nice of you to include me in your list of "Women I'd most like to see on the back of my Harley." The photo's not quite clear: is that a long-sleeved shirt or a tattoo?

Hey-Ho, Dr. Steve!

Please, not to worry about being late for lunch. Doctors get paged; have patients to tend to, even on their days off. I'm a nurse, I get it. I only wish I hadn't chosen that cozy window table because frankly, I could hardly breathe or taste the Gorgonzola on my salad due to the fumes rising from your body. Reminded me of inhaling at the Fillmore back in the day. And yeah, it's cool, it's legal, but you ran a close second to the lawyer I met for breakfast who'd apparently just bathed in Polo Blue. Thanks, but I'm going to pass on the offer to attend the all-day meditation session and vegan buffet at Stinson—my ironing's piling up.

Dear Wyatt:
What a lovely dinner. Thank for asking the maître d to seat us in the back so I could see the room—what a gorgeous restaurant. And thank you for telling the waitress that we'd let her know when we'd need her, that we were there to talk. Friday's fine. Six o'clock? Just bring yourself and oh, a little red wine.

Patience Training

Evelyn M. Zimmer

*Patience Training…*that is what he called it. *Bastard.* Vivian both fumed and chuckled wickedly as she remembered the evening he turned the tables on her.

The hunting lodge was to be deserted except for them. Ceafo saw to that, she knew her Mistress needed time alone with her lover. Having instructed the gamekeeper to have the kitchen stocked, the efficient and closed mouth man gave the rest of the orders to the housekeeper. The servants were to ready the lodge for an extended stay, and leave. Not to return until ordered. Walking swiftly to the stables, he checked on the boy, informing him that after the mounts were properly watered, fed and brushed down, he was to see to the gear… then stay in the stable. Period. He was a good boy, he would do as ordered, and he loved his mistress… poor child. The man prided himself on following orders, and he also liked the pleased look in Ceafo's eyes when he went above her call of duty.

Lady Vivian Bloodstrider sauntered into her hunting lodge and was pleased, removing her gloves she tossed them on the entrance table… moving gracefully and quickly towards the large stone fireplace, large enough to roast a couple of small humans if she ever got the chance… she warmed her hands and began running through her plans in her head… that is when she saw it.

The note was in his fine strong hand. Deliberate and to the point. Not what she was expecting. He left instructions for her. *For her!* "Humph," she was intrigued at the audacity… and she was in the mood to play…

"Lady Vivian, please put on the item I left for you. It is on the bed. Do not wear anything else." No signature was needed. Scrapping her plans for him, she was willing to roll with his game. *This time.*

She went up the stairs to the master bedchamber, her father's old rooms… very masculine, all animal heads, leather, and large dark furniture, a portrait of the former Bloodstrider hung above the large wooden desk on one side of the rather imposingly large room… then again, it was a hunting lodge. She loved this room. Her mother never came here, and of all her sisters, only Aureon enjoyed it as much as she. Then again, Aureon did follow the path of Diana and became a huntress. Vivian, on the other hand… followed yet a different path.

Unlacing her bracers as she approached the bed, she chuckled at the 'item' he left for her… such a piece of fluff would never hold up to the climate here. Turning her back to the bed, she propped herself against the footboard and began tugging at her boots… hopping a bit as she tried to keep her balance and then tossed them towards the corner. She rubbed her feet quickly, relishing the freedom. She was glad she didn't wear her heavy gear that she normally wore up here. But again, this was a different kind of hunting. A slight thirst started to hum along her nerve endings, dancing around the edges of her awareness.

Vivian always lamented the lack of a mirror up here when she was younger, innocent, a child… now, she was glad she couldn't see herself, what she has become. Turning away from the thought, she undid the clasp on her cloak, letting it drop, then thinking better of it, picked it up and went to the wardrobe to hang it up herself, court life really was spoiling her. Or rather, Ceafo had spoiled her.

Removing her chest piece and leg guards, she followed suit and hung them as well. They would be found when she left and then cleaned; they would be waiting for her on her return.

Unpinning her hair, she let it fall about her shoulders in thick dark blond waves, running her hands through it to loosen it further… finding the last of the pins. She wanders over to the smaller fireplace that keeps this chamber cozy. The bath is there, cooling, but still warm enough to remove the dirt from the road. Fresh, clean soap and thick towels are on hand as well. She stepped into the copper tub and sank down slowly, loving the feel of water on her flesh.

Feeling relaxed and unsoiled for a change, she drapes the towel on the nearby stool and struts naked to the window, looking out she sees the weather turning… a soft rain begins to pelt the panes of glass. A low chuckle emits from her throat as she thinks about how many times he gets caught in the rain. *Serves him right,* she thinks, *ordering me about…*

Turning to the inevitable, she approaches the 'item' with trepidation. Fluff was not her specialty. Seduction for her was more masculine… traditionally.

The hour is getting late, and she has stalled enough, *surely he must have arrived by now.* Patience was wearing thin. Thirst growing in equal amount to lust as she thinks of him wet, caught in the rain… grabbing the cloth, she pulls it over her head and is amazed at the softness of the fabric, how it hugs her without seeming to cling… to much… and the drape of the material… oh, how she loved voile. Shear yet not indecent… it flattered her curves beautifully, at least from what she could tell without a mirror. The sensual feel of the cloth only heightened her arousal.

Leaving the chamber, she went back down the stairs, fully aware of the cold stone beneath her bare feet. Passing through the large common room, she went to the kitchen area and found the platters of meat and fruit already arranged. Picking them up, she brought them to the table before the fireplace. Glancing about for the liquor cabinet, she finds what she requested. Bourbon. Plenty of it too. She grabs two short glasses and the bottle, then a second, and brings it to the table as well. She pours herself a glass, then one for him. Taking a piece of fruit, she pops it into her mouth and picks up her glass and takes a seat in the big leather club chair in front of the fireplace.

Then she sees it. Another note. Picking it up from the end table she reads it quickly.

"Vivian, wait."

Wait! Wait my… she stops herself from continuing the expletive. *This is a game,* she reminds herself. She can wait, for a short while… but he will pay for his impudence. Control has never been her strong suite. Control has not served her in a very long time. She was getting thirsty… and the bourbon was just adding fuel to an already smoldering fire.

As she waited, she studied the cut glass in her hand, the way the honey colored liquid dances with the light of the fireplace behind it, transforming it, shades of light and dark... not unlike her current mood. She swirled the liquid... she could smell it. Strong. Good. She needed something strong to help her with her control. *Concentrate on this liquid and not the other...the dark ruby, nearly black crimson, thick, sweet, slightly metallic, slightly salty... so much for control,* she chuckles.

Time passes as she waited for him... hunger and thirsts of all natures growing, building... testing her patience... pushing her control.

Sitting in the big leather club chair in front of the fire, she hears his footsteps behind her, his chest brushes against her shoulder as he reaches for his bourbon on the side table, sinking to a crouch behind her, his hand moved to her shoulder and began a sensual game of tease... leaning forward into the back of her neck, he nuzzled his chin just below her ear and whispered softly, "I'm home my pet..."

Her nipples stiffen, and her body floods the moment she hears the timber of his voice... deep, sensual... hungry... she keeps very still, allowing him to roam at his leisure.

As she softly moaned, she tilted her head to the side, and then back to rest against his chest... allowing him access to nuzzle... lick... and softly bite the very sensitive space between her neck and shoulder... soft groans began to take the form of a small pant...

Wetting her lips, her fangs descend, her breasts aching for his touch... every nerve taught as she schools herself to not move... to wait... to be patient...

Scared

DJ Tyrer

I stare at the mirror and wonder, yet again, if tonight is a terrible mistake. The face that looks back at me is like a clown's. Despite all the practice, I just can't get the makeup right. I place my hands palms down on the dressing table and try to slow my breathing. Beneath the over-applied blusher, I can feel my face growing numb; the beginning of a panic attack. I'm scared.

I grab a wipe and clean my face, then look back at the mirror.

"You can do this." I grab my eyeliner and begin to start again. *Lightly, lightly.*

It's strange that, despite everything, it's these little things that are both so vital and so difficult to master.

Then again, I never really imagined I'd be going on a date. Fantasized, of course, but never as something real.

My tummy's churning; a sensation I'm familiar with but hadn't expected to feel today. *Why am I so scared when everything seems to be going right?*

I suppose everyone feels like a fraud on a first date. It's just that it's how I've felt my whole life, and I shouldn't have to now.

I don't need to. He knows exactly who I am, has known right from the beginning; I never pretended otherwise.

I'm done. I stand and examine myself in the mirror, smooth my skirt straight. I sigh with relief. I look okay.

Oh, one last thing. Perfume. I bought a bottle especially for tonight. His favorite, I remember he mentioned it in one of his messages. Then I think, *Might he be offended? Is it in bad taste?* I spray it on anyway and pray I've done the right thing.

There's the sound of a car horn. *I'm late!* My cab is here.

I slip on my shoes, clatter down the stairs, grab my shawl and burst out along my garden path. I glance back to check that I shut my front door, then open that of the cab and slip inside.

"Where to?"

"Mario's." It's the only Italian restaurant in town, and everyone knows it.

The ride is just long enough that I'm starting to panic again by the time we arrive, but not long enough for me to ask him to turn around.

"That'll be eight-fifty," he says.

I thrust a ten at him and tell him to keep the change. I step out and find myself in front of Mario's. I half-turn, but the cab is already pulling away. I could still walk away…

No. Deep breaths. *I want this, no matter what my thumping pulse is telling me.*

I step up to the door, push it open and step inside. A pleasant smell insinuates its way into my nostrils, and the clatter and hubbub of the diners wash over me. The experience is an alien one.

Okay, it's not really that posh, but I'm only really used to takeaways.

I step up to the counter.

"Amanda Shire, guest of Mr. Dean. Uh, Robert Dean." I find it hard, still, to think of him as anything other than as a 'mister.'

"Ah, yes, table fourteen." The maitre d'—is that the right term here?—passes me on to a waiter, who leads me towards the rear of the restaurant. I'm glad… Robert listened when I asked him to book one there; I'd hate sitting by the window, feeling as if I'm on display to be judged by passersby.

I see him; he is studying the menu and hasn't noticed me yet. It's the first time I've seen him, face-to-face, in nearly two decades and he hardly seems to have changed; only his salt-and-pepper hair is now white. I, on the other hand, have changed completely.

He looks up as we near the table.

"Amanda!" He smiles and stands, takes my shawl, then pulls back a chair and seats me. Nobody's ever done anything like that for me before. This is real.

He sits down, and the waiter passes me a menu.

"What would you recommend?" I ask my date. Spag bol is about the extent of my knowledge of Italian food and wine is only red or white as far as I'm concerned.

Robert makes a suggestion, and I nod, so he gives the waiter our order and the man bustles off.

I start when Robert reaches out and takes my hands.

"It's good to see you," he says.

I smile nervously back, not really sure how to proceed. I've been on precisely one previous date in my life, about twenty years ago, and that was a disaster. I feel as if I'm deluding myself, coming here.

"It's good to see you, too. You look just like I remember you."

Mr. Dean was my teacher. I'm not sure I ever learned much geography. I fancied him, then. I paid plenty of attention to him, but not to what he was saying.

It's the same now. I'm staring at him, but not taking in a word he's saying.

"I'm sorry. I was just…"

He chuckles. "Don't apologize. I was just saying how nice you look."

"Really?"

"Really," he says with a smart nod. Robert still has that military bearing I remember so well, like a hero from an old movie. I know I can trust him when he says that.

"I think it's a really brave thing you've done, Amanda, and I'd love to share the life you're building for yourself."

That's not as presumptuous as it sounds; we've been in contact online, messaging one another and skyping, for the last year or so. Still, I feel my heart skip a beat at the implication in his words.

After the operation, as I reassessed my life, I found my mind turning back to my schooldays. I hadn't really kept in contact with anyone from back then, but I suddenly found myself interested in what they'd been doing. I suppose I was hoping, mainly, for a little schadenfreude, at the expense of those who were mean to me. In the course of my nostalgia, I'd remembered Mr. Dean and looked him up, then, on impulse, sent him a friend request.

I never imagined we'd reach this point. I'm not really sure what I was thinking. Probably, it was the hardest thing I'd had to do since telling my mother. He, of course, had known me as John. But, he wasn't bothered, was supportive.

Robert had recently retired and had lost his wife a few years earlier and, as he supported me, I was there for him. And, as they say, one thing led to another, and he asked me out…

Our wine arrived and our food shortly after.

"Maybe we should discuss the weather," I say.

He laughs, and I feel relief that my joke hasn't fallen flat. Our small talk is atrocious. Neither of us has had many friends, so it doesn't come easily.

"I'm sorry," he says, "Margaret and I… But, you don't want me discussing my late wife on our date."

"I don't mind, honestly." I sigh. "What do people say on dates like this?"

"I'm afraid it's not really my area of expertise. I think we know one another, now, too well to talk as strangers, but not well enough to converse as friends."

I wish I had some news to impart, but neither of us is doing much these days; in my case, because nobody will hire me. In fact, he is one of the few people who, when they know about me, treat me as a person, not a thing.

The waiter approaches as soon as we finish our meal and takes our order for dessert.

We eat in silence for a time and, while I love just being with him, I have a horrible sinking feeling inside of me that the date is turning into a failure.

Suddenly, Robert puts down his spoon and looks at me. I freeze with my spoon halfway to my mouth; his intense gaze disconcerting. I feel a little comical.

Slowly, I lower my spoon and say, "Yes?"

"When was the last time you had a vacation?"

"Not counting my time in hospital, I would have to say it was when I went away with my parents when I was fifteen." It always came back to that period twenty years ago.

"I never had a good job," I add, apologetically, as if admitting something terrible, "and then I was saving for the cost of my operation, so…"

"How would you like to go away with me?"

"Sorry?"

"We could go away somewhere, or take a cruise. I haven't been away since… well, a few years. There's little point to going alone. So, how about it? Separate rooms, of course," he adds; "unless…"

It was my turn to reach out and grip his hands. "I'd love to! Oh, you have no idea how much I'd love to…"

"Then, might I suggest we retire to your flat to discuss it further?"

"Lets!" It would be the perfect end to the evening and, I hope, the beginning of a whole new life in which I could finally be myself and be loved for it.

I didn't feel scared anymore.

Talking About The Tudors

Mike Evis

What is she talking about now? Alan absently stroked his beard, quickly stopping himself—that dating guide he'd read said it was a bad sign of nerves. Instead, he moved his hand down and stroked his beer glass. That ought to be safe enough, the guide hadn't mentioned inanimate objects.

He still felt like a bag of nerves, but at least conversation wasn't a problem. She could talk for England, hardly pausing for breath before continuing. Talk, talk, talk. No, the only problem he had was concentrating on what she was saying, rather than letting his mind drift off. *Something about the Tudors? That was it.*

"Sorry," he muttered, remembering too late that the guide had said not to mumble. 'Speak clearly and assertively,' it said. 'Listen attentively, when you're not speaking.' He was failing on both of those, all right. Even at school, he'd never been able to concentrate for too long. Sooner or later his thoughts would wander off. It never took much for him to start daydreaming or thinking about something else.

"What did you say?" he said, a little louder.

At least he remembered her name—*Julia, wasn't it?* She looked unfazed as if used to people drifting off whilst she spoke. *I bet she is,* he thought, smiling to himself, *the amount she talks.*

"I was just saying in school I hated history, but now I'm really interested in the Tudors, all that period, it's fascinating, don't you agree? I can't get enough of it. I loved '*The Other Boleyn Girl,*' and I was completely hooked on '*Wolf Hall.*'"

He nodded. It didn't seem to matter what he said, really, as long as he showed some interest, said 'yeah,' or 'uh-huh,' she still kept talking, ten to the dozen.

He was fascinated, captivated in fact, but not by what she was saying, the words just washed over him like so much background noise, no, it was her he was captivated by. There she sat, long fair hair hanging down well below the neckline of her white patterned blouse, top few buttons undone to show a touch of cleavage, her skin tanned a rich, deep golden brown. When she got animated, waving her hands about and shifting in her chair, he couldn't take his eyes off her breasts as they moved in sympathy. There was so much to admire about her. There was her mouth, vivid red lips, so luscious, parting to reveal perfect white teeth, and when she smiled, her smile radiated out across her face, as if she were inviting him to go further. Then there were those dark black eyes, expressively widening as she spoke, and her hands, like the rest of her, as smooth as a baby's skin—*no rings,* he noticed—spread out on the table towards him. She was absolutely gorgeous.

Walking down towards the Half Moon Inn earlier, Alan hadn't had a good feeling about this date. The pub was her suggestion, but it was an area of town he usually kept clear of, near the old docks. Narrow streets were full of run down and derelict buildings, shops long closed, terraced houses boarded up, and groups of dubious looking youths standing around. At the end of the street, twenty yards beyond the pub, flowed the filthy old river, lending the whole area a ripe stench of decay.

It certainly wasn't somewhere he'd normally go at night. So he'd been in two minds when he came to the Half Moon—though the pub wasn't derelict, it had seen better days—it was the sort of place where you could imagine blokes being 'sorted out', stolen property being fenced, drug deals taking place, and all manner of dodgy dealings. It didn't seem the most obvious place for a blind date. He'd go in, *but if I really didn't like the look of the place—or her—I'll leave*, he thought. But when he walked in and saw her sitting there, he swept all those thoughts from his mind. *Wow*, he thought, *a woman like her you could dream about for all eternity*. But it would be too much to hope for, wouldn't it, that this woman sitting there in a short skirt could be his date? On the website, her profile said she was thirty, but this woman looked far younger.

"Are you…?"

"Julia. Hi. You must be Alan."

He had no further thoughts of walking out of the pub. And his usual worries over what to talk about weren't an issue either. He didn't need to say anything, she kept talking, and he listened. Well, to be honest, not exactly listening, more sitting there, dazzled by her sheer beauty. And he wasn't the only one, either.

The men standing at the bar kept shooting glances over their way every now and again. *Tough,* he thought, *she's my date.* Idle thoughts, like the clouds drifting over on a summer's day, went through his mind. *What would it be like to sink into her arms,* he wondered. Each time, he told himself: *Stop, you're racing too far ahead of yourself, you'll only be disappointed, remember those other dates.* But no sooner would he dismiss one than another day dream entered his head. There was little doubt, though, even if she did rabbit on forever, she was far less crazy than some he'd met. And it was far less nerve racking if you didn't have to worry about making conversation.

What a collection of weirdos some of his past dates had been! He'd almost given up hope, it seemed there were no normal women out there at all. *One more time,* he had told himself, *I'll give it one more shot, and then...*

There was the girl who was a yoga instructor and wanted him to try out some yoga positions right there in the wine bar. He'd hardly been able to move for days after that. And then there was that short, dark haired women, who sat there in silence for about three-quarters of an hour, no matter how much he tried to make conversation, before suddenly bursting into tears and running out of the restaurant. And that other woman who disappeared to the ladies after half an hour, and never came back. He hadn't seen that coming. They seemed to be getting on well, but then she'd taken a phone call, and gone to the loo, and that was that. Perhaps tonight he could forget all about them because he was sure this Julia wasn't like that.

She wasn't crazy, well, aside from her obsession with the Tudors, and she was definitely interested in him. All right, she did talk a lot, but it saved him having to think of things to say, he was never any good at that. This way he didn't need to say much at all, just let her gabble on. And if she was interested in him, well, he was definitely interested. He found his thoughts drifting, imagining slipping his hand inside her blouse…

His thoughts had run away with him again.

"It was a violent time all right-," she was saying.

Phew, that was okay. He hadn't missed anything, she was still going on about the Tudors. But how could he think about Tudor England when he was sitting opposite a woman like this? He watched her fingers sliding up and down her glass, her nails painted a deep crimson. Her lips painted the same color, distracted him from grasping her words.

"… blood…," she said. "So much blood." More about the Tudors, he guessed. His hand went up towards his chin, but he checked himself in time. *Don't blow it now,* he thought. He could only hope she hadn't realized he hadn't been listening. Could she really be as interested in him as he was in her? Well, surely she wouldn't be talking so much if she wasn't, would she? Her dark mascaraed eyes were locked on him—that had to be a good sign, didn't it? He felt himself blushing and felt the stares of the men at the bar. *They know,* he thought, *that she's the most attractive woman in here.*

She hadn't asked him much about himself, though. There'd hardly been a chance. And she hadn't really told him much about herself either. Just went on and on about the Tudors all the time. *Is that all she ever talks about? Well, there could be worse things. Really, what does it matter? You can't be fussy with a woman like this.* Everyone had their minor faults. But as soon as you laid eyes on her you'd want her. That explained the hungry eyes from the blokes at the bar, hovering there like a pack of wolves seeking their prey. But he was keeping them at bay.

"That's good," she suddenly said. "You haven't been put off yet."

What? Has she finally stopped talking about the Tudors? Out of the corner of his eye, he saw a rough looking, unshaven bloke in a leather jacket, bit older than him, give him a leering grin as if to say, 'blimey, has she finally shut up?' He nodded to the bloke, but all he did was just grin wider.

He quickly turned back to her—God, he certainly didn't want to appear uninterested, not the way things were going.

"No," he said, "not all all. How could I be put off? It was… fascinating."

He just hoped she didn't quiz him about what she'd said. He didn't imagine she would, but if she did it would be like doing history at school, at the end of the lesson, when the teacher went round the class, asking questions about the facts he'd imparted, and Alan realized he had no idea what the lesson had been about. He hated that feeling, knowing he knew nothing, the way they all laughed when he said the Spanish Armada had gone off to discover America.

But there was nothing to worry about here. Her eyes widened, a smile spread across her face and with a bronzed hand she reached across the table to hold his hand. He felt an electric tingle. All those useless dates, and now this. This was his reward, and it was almost too incredible. For a delicious instant, nothing existed but the depths of her eyes and the warm touch of her fingers stroking his.

"Good," she said. "It's so nice when… You won't believe all the bad experiences I've had doing this. I'd almost given up."

"Me too," he said.

"So many men just run off when I tell them."

"Really?" He shook his head. "Incredible, isn't it?"

"I know. They just don't want to know."

"That's… I can't believe that."

"But I think it's only right, to be honest from the outset."

"Absolutely," he said. "It's best to be straight about things." *You'd agree to anything,* he thought, *with a woman like this.* "You know," he carried on, "it's such a relief to meet someone, and I hope this doesn't sound rude, who's normal. I've met some strange people on other dates."

"Tell me about it," she said and smiled. "If I told you about some of the people I've met."

Was he imagining it, or was the bloke in the leather jacket grinning at him again?

"One bloke said I needed help, but he didn't want to get involved."

"That's so rude."

"That's what I thought! But that's why I spend some time talking to people, making sure they understand first. You're sure you're quite okay about it?" She squeezed his hand.

"I suppose a lot just won't understand," he said.

She stroked his hand again.

"Thank you. I can't tell you what this means to me." She let out a deep sigh.

"I suppose it is… unusual," he said.

Someone at the bar guffawed loudly.

"So many just can't handle it."

She lowered her head, and he admired her neck, like the rest of her it was beautiful too, smooth and tanned, just an occasional fair hair here and there. She was perfect. How lucky he was, to have found this lovely woman tonight. He imagined kissing that smooth skin, well, maybe he would soon…

"I suppose it is a bit out of the ordinary? But we're all different," he said.

"That's what I thought," she said, looking back up again. "But you," she said, gazing directly at him. "You're just one in a million. I'm so glad. You don't judge, and you don't—"

Her other hand moved over and lightly touched his shoulder.

"Well, it's their loss," he said.

"It's strange, though," she said. "The other men I met seemed very interested to begin with, but then they'd suddenly lose interest. Now, you've got to be really honest here, are you really sure you're not put off? You don't think I'm damaged?"

"No, of course not."

"And you're… you're really fine with what I told you?"

"Absolutely." *Why on earth would I be bothered over her interest in the Tudors?* He'd cheerfully watch her sitting there reading out the telephone directory, he thought. It was understandable, her being a bit cautious when you thought of all those bad dates she'd had.

"I know I talk a lot."

"Really, it's okay."

"I think this is going really well," she said. "I'm so pleased I saw your profile on the website. I thought when I read it, you sounded understanding and sympathetic, just the sort of guy I could really talk to."

"Like I said, it doesn't matter to me what your interests are."

A furrow of puzzlement wrinkled her forehead but quickly disappeared again.

"So, would you like…" he was sure her voice was wavering "…to come back for a coffee?"

As she spoke, he heard the pub door crash open and bang against the wall so loudly it shook for several long seconds. It was followed by someone stomping in. *Must be some drunk*, he thought and ignored it. People were constantly coming and going, and what else mattered at this moment, other that the way the date was going, sitting opposite this beautiful woman, who'd just invited him back. Her hands were still entwined with his. *What a fantastic evening!* He'd long given up hope any of his dates could ever work out. He couldn't imagine a date could go this well.

"Love to come back—" he started to say, but something had gone wrong with his throat. It felt like a vice was clamped hard around it, and he could hardly breathe. His words struggled to come out as a faint gasp. *God, am I having a stroke or a heart attack?* The symptoms seemed to fit, especially as he couldn't move either, he couldn't even turn round. He could just hear the blokes at the bar all laughing their heads off. Seemed bad taste to him, looking on and laughing when someone was being taken ill. And sounded like one of them was taking photos too. *Why don't they call an ambulance?* God, wasn't this just great timing when he was getting on so well with Julia? And although she did look worried, she was also oddly frozen, her eyes focussed somewhere behind him.

The pressure eased, and he found he could turn his head slightly. As he did so, he saw two giant, hairy hands planted one on each side of his shoulder. Tattooed on one knuckle was the word 'HATE,' on the other it said 'LOVE.'

"I've told you before!" boomed a loud voice right behind his ear. "But you don't listen! You keep doing it!"

The grip loosened a bit further, just one hand resting heavily on his shoulder. Alan was now able to turn and look round properly. A shaven-headed giant of a man, six foot six tall and as solid as a brick outhouse stood behind him, covered in tattoos all over his shoulder and both arms… and did that one with a snake curled round two hearts say 'JULIA' or was he misreading it?

Alan quivered, realizing the giant only had to lift his little finger to flatten him.

"So. I turn my back, and this is what happens." The man glared at Alan with bloodshot eyes full of hate.

"We were just—" said Alan.

"You! Shut up! I'm talking to my wife."

Something queasy went through Alan's stomach.

"Ex-wife," said Julia quickly.

"Not in the eyes of God you're not."

"I do what I like with my life now."

"Not while I'm around," said the giant, spitting loudly on the floor.

He turned to Alan.

"And with this… this puny specimen? Look at him."

He squeezed Alan's arm, painfully.

"There's nothing there. No muscle, nothing."

He let go, shaking his head.

Julia's eyes were full of sadness as she looked at Alan.

"I'm sorry about this. But it was bound to happen sooner or later, as I said. And I know you do understand after I told you all about it."

Now the giant's grip tightened again on his shoulder.

"But I thought you were talking about the Tudors?" said Alan.

She looked puzzled.

"The Tudors? Did I? I might have mentioned 'Wolf Hall,' but… No, I was talking about Kevin, how I left him, and how he simply won't accept it, won't leave me alone. I was telling you all about his drunken rages, the violence."

"Violent am I! We'll see about violence!" shouted the giant.

"Kevin, please."

"He's leaving… now!"

Thick hands prised under his armpits and he realized he was being lifted out of his chair. There was no way he could resist. Then, before he knew it, he was propelled through the open pub door, landing with a painful thud on the wet, cold paving slabs in the street. The last thing he heard before the door slammed shut was the sound of further raucous laughter, and Julia shouting out to him.

"But I thought you understood."

The Mockingbird

W. P. Osborn

The dark things Nonny McGuiness has been wearing lately are dressed up today with pendant earrings and one of her mother's nice scarves. As she comes into school, her step is firm, and her posture straighter and anyone who knows her will be struck by a fresh keenness of eye. So at midday, sure enough, one of the boys, wearing a creamy V-neck, white slacks, and sneakers, falls in line to walk with her. It's Dieter Becker. Dieter is captain of the tennis team. He straddles the cafeteria bench beside her, hugging himself, pooching his lips out, not looking over the pandemonium of the student lunch anymore, but rolling his eyes back like a dead man and bellowing, "Really big shoe."

Nonny indicates her mouth, which is full of broccoli and cheese, and he goes, "Wool. Wool. Thot'sh all right now." Then he punches her in the arm. "Jimmy Stewart," he says—"Get it?"

He mimics, it turns out, almost exclusively. He claims forty distinctive sets of voice and gesture and to be working on more. If she doesn't know one, it's her fault. She gushes over his talent.

"I'm Spartacus," he's insisting. "Are ye Spartacus? Oy thought oy was Spartacus."

He leans in. He says, "Now I ask you Nonny, who would want to be Spartacus?"

In the succeeding minutes Nonny identifies Joe Hardy and Superman, and by the lifted brow and the florid sheen of his face, she knows she pleases him.

"You're awfully intelligent, aren't you ma'am?" he asks flatly. As she answers, "Dragnet," it dawns on her she's received a compliment.

"I'm a senior," he adds, apparently back in his natural voice.

"That's great!" she exclaims.

As she stands, she feels tall and gawky, but he clucks his tongue and winks up at her, and his eyes are serene, and wow is it hard to tell him she's got to get to Speech!

★★★★

Thursday after supper she's sent to the kitchen for the phone. The voice on the line is husky, but it's not impersonating, and it doesn't belong to Dieter Becker. This happens to be one Kendall Roberts, who begins, "Remember me? I saw you."

Kendall's the kid whose eyes she locked onto last Friday at the football game, the first boy she's ever made any real contact with in her life, and the reason for her vivaciousness at the beginning of the week. Over the weekend, the more she remembered his open mouth and serious expression, the more trouble she had with homework and with sleep. On Monday, however, arriving the same moment as he did for first-period Algebra, when she shrugged her shoulders at him and smiled, he got red, wouldn't hold her gaze, and edged past her like she was in the way!

"So," he says now, "would you want to do something?"

She says perversely, "I do things all the time."

"Tuh, I mean together," he stammers.

"No. Um, wha'd you have in mind?"

"A show, I guess. We could eat before. You know—burgers like."

She curls a lock of her hair around her finger and imagines him in his plaid shirt and corduroys, his peculiar green sneakers.

"Tomorrow night," he goes on.

"Have to check."

She puts down the phone and makes herself hum 'Life Is but a Dream.' She knows from personal experience what his want for her must be like, so it's not that she can't empathize. It's just that for making her wait six days to hear from him, he ought to be made to suffer. Besides, when it rains it pours, and she's got Dieter Becker to think of now.

"We're busy," she tells him.

"Saturday then."

"Nope, booked."

"Fuh, next Friday?"

How engaged can she pretend to be? She toe-taps a plank of the wooden floor. "Well," she says, "not burgers, though, okay?" Then she drops the handset back into the cradle, revolted at her female weakness.

He rings the doorbell eleven minutes late. He tells Father he had trouble finding the correct address. Here the young couple are then, striding up Sea Road, the earliest moments of the only real engagement Nonny's ever been out on, and she's already fuming about a lie. She knows he lied because at twenty to six her sister reported there was a boy outside looking at his watch, slicking his hair, checking his barn door.

But pizza and ginger ale begin to relax her and to keep things moving she describes the inside of her English teacher Miss Bauer's cottage, where she's recently been for an essay conference. She tells Kendall how she accidentally oversweetened her tea, how when she threw it outside there was this rabbit she didn't see, it was in this bush? and she managed to scald it possibly because it shot out of there so fast.

"I hope the ants didn't find it," he responds reasonably. "They can scent sugar at three hundred feet, you know."

Their talk stops.

He goes, "So how about our football team?"

She answers, "I honestly don't really care that much about football."

Another lapse. Now they both speak. "Sorry," she says.

"No, you."

"You."

"Well if you weren't at the game," he argues, "then how'd we end up on a date together?"

"I just went the once," she says, and she thinks about the word date, which is a time, and an event, and a person, and a fruit. "My mother made me."

The movie they end up attending is set in the South American rainforest. Romance cannot ignite there because the European couple are surrounded by too many of their pygmy hosts. About half way through, Kendall begins, in increments, to lean toward her. Finally, it's near the end. Outsiders have come to mine the rich gold deposits, and the tribe has to find a new place to live or else face the complete loss of its traditional way of life. Somewhat remediating the sadness of their conundrum is the fact that as a result, Egbert and Julianne will finally have the opportunity to obtain a little privacy. Having decided not to go along with the pygmies on their migration deeper into the jungle, they will head off on their own.

The swing of her hair, the glint of his teeth, the sunlit sheet and bead of the river they stand in by themselves up to the waist. Through the murk can be seen the gathering of robust-looking small fish with underbites. Flamenco guitar music comes in underwater, while on the surface it's just the natural sounds of the insects and birds and breeze to accompany the closing together of the two principals. Kendall's been leaning on her for half an hour, and Nonny is sweltering. Egbert's got Julianne in his arms, but there are many more of the fish now. The river is shown again from above. No one is present in it or on the shore either. As the fish disperse, Nonny sees the murk in the water as being possibly tinged with red. Then, as the credits roll, there is a long view of a man leading a woman through a clearing and toward the edge of the forest. Nonny's relieved for their safety, though in the way of an ending she feels incompletely satisfied.

She and Kendall stroll out from under the marquee into the cool Lindo Mar night. When she accidentally bumps him, their hands touch and she locks his fingers before he can draw away. "Man-eating piranha," he says then.

"Pardon me?"

"Those fish in the river," he says. "They'll pick your bones in ninety seconds."

★★★★

Before Algebra, looking at his feet, he tells her he had fun. She returns in kind.

May he phone her again then?

She's so busy.

Yes, but may he?

She recalls the football stadium a few weeks ago, the way the place went mute, the gaze that for such a startling moment linked them both together. Half reluctantly she accedes. But when he calls again, she can't help joshing him, shrouding the fact that she's locked down now on the lank hair and heavy-lidded eyes of Dieter Becker—has gotten herself into a five-days-a-week enthrallment which, when she reflects on it at night, so makes her want to laugh.

In English she finds herself standing, swaying on her feet. You're pale, the frowning Miss Bauer tells her—report to the nurse tout de suite.

She drifts up to Kit Carson Hall feeling like a helium balloon. She turns the corner nearest her locker. Stops. In the semi-dark of the nook for the fire hose are two students. One of them is that black-haired Penny Donegal. The other props himself against the wall, caging the girl between his arms and saying, "Oshk naught what your country con do for you."

Nonny's walking backward, her knees water instead of bone, her cramp winching tighter. When she bends over and retches, Dieter says, "Oh Rochester," and puts his palm to his cheek like Jack Benny. She's sitting on the floor now, kneading her midriff, Penny D. squatting beside her and saying, "Your compact broke, sorry, sorry," and returning what spilled into Nonny's handbag. "It's your time?"

she whispers. "Can I get you anything? Is there something you want me to do?"

Nonny climbs to her feet. Her knees and ankles tremble. Her head pounds at the center. She unlocks her locker, fumbles out her emergency kit, and weaves off for the girls' room. Her skirt smells, she discovers. The back of it is damp and darkly smirched with hall grime. When the lunch bell finally rings, faint and far away, she's past the temporary classrooms, off campus, a block and a half toward home.

★★★★

Kendall proposes they bus to Tijuana. "Bullfights," he says. "Toro toro."

"No, no," Nonny laughs. "But we could get together again if you still wanted to."

He blurts something about Dieter Becker. In refusing to discuss her private business, she manages not to reveal that she has been finished with Dieter for a week now. For some reason, she doesn't want to be overheard. Her parents are in the living room, reading. Crystal's in the den watching 'Route 66.' The blood courses up into her face. "Yes," she half-whispers. "I'll see you on Friday night if you like."

Father's got a conference in Los Angeles. Mother and Crystal are up at the school supporting Lindo High's Baleen Whales as they contest for the league football title. Nonny's got absolute mountains of homework, she's said, and has begged off going with. That is why she and Kendall are able to occupy a nook at the foot of the sandstone bluff at Hansen's Break. She's thought to bring along a blanket; he has thought to bring along corn chips. It's so dark she can barely see him, but she can hear him munching. Fingers touch her face, then move to her shoulder.

"Chesterfield King?" he asks. When she doesn't reply, he says, "They're my dad's. Me, I don't smoke. Hey, here—what about a cookie?"

She holds in check the impulse she has to pull him close to settle him. Suddenly in front of her is an under-lighted evil-looking face that makes her gasp. When he shines the beam in her eyes, she refuses to squint, so when he switches it off again, she gets a persistent green afterglow. Warm air puffs across her neck, now, and she's kissed. Nothing touches her but his lips. It is the first time ever, and it's interesting the way want and reception link. But it is also dryer than she thinks it might be, and as it's mostly between the nose and mouth, it seems off kilter.

"Sweet," she says, and she touches his hair and kisses him back, demonstrating a softer, moister way. He twists and bears down. Her scalp and eyes prickle, but she dabs his upper lip with her tongue, and it's like he almost gets it, because he swishes along her teeth now. When he jabs a little into her mouth, and she pivots aside, he asks her what's wrong. His whiskers are like an emery board. It would be better if he were smooth like Miss Bauer. She decides to help him try again. This time, his lips begin to conform. He's massaging her shoulders, and she preens, her eyes closing when he goes under her coat. His stroke broadens and begins to include the soft places under her arms.

Back at the cottage the afternoon Miss Bauer held her, Nonny shuddered out a sound, apparently the combined result of emotional risk and bodily pleasure. She's not going to let that happen here.

Mother calls the public display of affection low and exhibitionist. Father's less judgmental about it, but he doesn't say Mother's wrong. Nonny herself has been repulsed by the writhing going on along the side walls of the Shore Theater—though in her room she's imagined herself in similar peril with certain boys in her classes.

His thumb traces the base of her breast, but it's accidental and just the once, so she lets her involuntary jump act as her retort. He says that twisting sideways is uncomfortable and he falls away. If it were daytime, she'd join him prone, because her shoulder's sore. But it's nighttime, and lying down— well she knows where to set her limits. She rolls to her knees, bends over, and covers his mouth again. His lips are softer, and his tongue is calmer, but without him right against her, her front's exposed. Better not risk his hands. As the safer alternative, she's beside him on her back, then.

There are no clouds, and she tries to focus on the stars, but they are obscured by the spray coming off the sea. Kendall takes her hand. He says it's nice— meaning, she sees, that for him it's more than just the kissing, that under his ardor are genuine feelings for her as a person. She knows what she won't permit, but she also feels she's taken at her worth. When she rolls toward him, there's an instant's hesitation, then the wetness of a kiss again, and she is shocked, a quick pulse through the skin as on the right side she is simply cupped. Her fist clenches, only the spreading thickening there is exquisite, and the punch she throws is more like a hard caress with her knuckles across his cheek and up through his hair. He pulls half the blanket over them, and now it's even all right when he goes under her blouse. She's on her knees again, coat off, her brassiere unfastened for easier access.

He palpates, he jiggles, he goes down her side. She wants to laugh, mostly tickled, but she makes herself cleave to his mouth. He's past her navel, a limit she can dispense with, but now under her belt, which she cannot. Touch them with his lips, she wants to feel it, has imagined it with others. Instead, he sucks on her neck. Her waist is drawn fast, then loosened, and her snap pops. Which is not too far if he'll just keep it at that.

His kisses, the warmth under the blanket, the weight of his hand on her stomach are so brand new. He slides over the top of her panties. Now he's resting. They're hardly kissing. She has wanted, yes, but wanting's not reality, and this is. Just in time, she grips his wrist. She moves him firmly to her breast and holds him there. Then, breathing more deeply, she slides her arm around him. His leg eases over her thigh. He's moving his hips against her. His hand starts down again, but she grabs it. She grants him her sternum, asserting once again her definite firm boundary, an indication of what she will and will not let him do. What is the hour? If she doesn't get back, she'll have to invent an untruth. But Dieter Becker's gone, fantasized others are out of the picture, Kendall Roberts is telling her, without speaking, things she's never heard, and the longer they remain, the more she feels connected. She wants him to want her, in truth wants to have happen exactly what he does. But oh is it dangerous! Take care of yourself girl, because the boys won't. So says Mother, and Father doesn't disagree.

His arm slithers.

"Kendall, darn it!"

This comes out in an urgent whisper. She hauls his hand up, squeezes and rubs it for a quarter of a minute or more, but when she releases it, he must be gravity, because down he goes again.

Honey here—not here.

Huh-uh!

She stills his hand where it's landed, but it pulses and paths of warmth run up behind her eyes. She shakes his wrist, but this only makes it worse. Her head expands, her grasp releases, her arms fall down to her sides.

"Ay!" she exclaims a moment later.

"What!"

"Fingernail?"

She turns, and his hand comes out—thank goodness because she's all but done for. He grinds against her front. She reciprocates almost involuntarily. When she slides her hand inside his shirt and strokes his back, his body goes rigid, and the breath chokes in his throat, and he goes, "Hold it! Geez! Don't! Don't!

"Not!" he wheezes. "Not!"

Are they found? What! What is it!

He's completely on top of her now, his head sideways, hips seeming to fight off a kind of vibration overtaking his whole body. It reminds her of what happened with Miss Bauer, only she knows she's way past Miss Bauer because with Miss Bauer she was involved, whereas with Kendall it's almost like she's watching it all. She thinks to coo him, to say his name. He doesn't speak. When he's too heavy, she touches his cheek and shifts him off. And now she's abandoned.

Remaining behind in the blanket is a scent which is kind of corny and sweet. It's not from the chips he brought. She's trying to figure out exactly what it is, and then she's got it. Girls in the sixth grade know this. You have to put two and two together! Or rather one and one, she thinks. And with Miss Bauer, it was nearly the same! For gosh sake! Miss Bauer!

He returns. His feet are coated with damp sand, but it doesn't matter, because all at once she's so completely aware of the mystifying contrast of a broken wave against the darkness, the familiar chop and pound of the surf farther out, the slide of the water coming in up the beach. She throws her arms around him and kisses him. She explores his tailbone. The swoop of the canyon there gets her giddy, and she works up the courage to reach around front. At the tepid moist thing that rolls across her palm, she blushes so hard her face stings, but a voice inside tells her to stay where she is, and she lets it bend and squirm in her hand. It has a kind of resiliency she's unfamiliar with. "Man," Kendall murmurs.

The effect she has on him would seem to be an extension of what happened on the night she first noticed him at the stadium. And there is warmth in her knowledge of his having ground against her and done—what did one call it? Their kisses now are of a different kind—physical, yes, but also more emotional. She undoes her blouse and pulls his head down. It makes her scowl, the quiet suckling he takes up there.

His kisses become undirected. She lets his hand glide where it wants to, pretends his thumb in her panties is without purpose even though she's got to lift her hips to help him get them down and, along with her denims, off. He pets her. The blanket prickles, yet its insinuation between her knees and buttocks, the drape of it over her naked hip, are parts of a special kind of intimacy. She brushes him with the back of her hand, finds an astonishing new heft there, and wonders truly how it's to be accommodated.

He's kicking his trousers off. When he's back beside her, it's something beyond the combined warmth of their nakedness, a provocative electricity running between his skin and hers, so that while she could still quit, the reason she'd want to has gone into the background. She can feel the hair and his—dare she think the name?—warmer than the rest of him, the penis that not a quarter of an hour ago discharged so near her skin! That he'd then washed off in the surf and that had afterward been so strange to her touch.

They're kissing again. The inside of her hums and she presses his hip, which she imagines is like signaling a horse to turn. He lifts himself on top again, and she feels him slide down her belly. He's pushing between her legs now. She cannot think how it will go.

"Lower?"

"Yes please," she answers.

She's got her legs together to help keep him centered. But he's as far as he can reach. This is it, then, the pressing there. Sex.

"Muh—maybe this is wrong," he says.

"I think you should have brought that up earlier!"

"I meant…"

"Kendall?"

"You know. We could—"

He's pushing her thigh out. She crosses her ankles and clamps her knees, want subsiding as the moment runs away from perfection. By game's end, she's got to set herself up for the appearance of study, too—beat Mother and Crystal back to the house.

"No," she says.

He doesn't stop.

She goes, "What're you doing?"

"This is how," he says.

"How what?"

He kisses her, but she doesn't feel affection.

"How," he repeats.

"I don't think so."

"Seen a picture."

"Sure you have."

But she doesn't have a better idea, and she lets him position her. He's doing something up and down with his hand. Then there's the pressure again. It feels to her pretty much like a chicken bone might. Is this what the other girls secretly smile over?

She squeezes her eyes shut. It may be how after all because as he rams, she's parting. But the why of it. The only feeling she can compare it to is having bad trouble on the toilet.

She opens her eyes, makes out through the blur of her weeping his dark form against the misted sky. His moaning seems more than one voice, the urge in him like the urge of the little grunion fish which on certain nights wriggle up on this sand to fertilize and bury their eggs. His shuddering comes on again. It feels as powerful as the first time, and she breathes in tiny puffs to try and lessen the pinching.

It stops. He rolls to his back. She tries to settle herself, only her mind runs over the injury. And if she was overdue before, how late must she be now? What will she say, how to explain the mess her clothes will be? Should she wash here in the salt water, or wait and use the shower?

Over the roar of the ocean comes a new sound, a mixing of intermittent musical tones. When she shakes her lover's shoulder, he throws a dead arm across her breast.

"Kendall!" she whispers.

The waves obscure it, but it's like the school orchestra tuning before an assembly. Gray beams shine over them into the surf. A motor guns; tires skitter. She's up on her knees again to find out what it is. It's cars. They're passing by above. Voices howl. Someone yells, "Nonnee!"

She realizes when she hears other shouts that it's not "Nonny." It's "Baleeeenn!"

Kendall, getting dressed now, exclaims, "Well all right!"

She wants to do something with him to seal in permanence whatever tonight should mean. But he isn't with her anymore. Not like he was.

When she's got her clothes back on, she pats him on the bottom, shrugs her shoulders, and turns and scrambles up the bank, projecting herself as she must into the role of a schoolgirl walking home following a championship football game. People whoop in the cold night air and rumble by. One car crawls up beside her. An impossible number of heads and arms and legs poke out of the windows. Perhaps ten boys, none of whom she recognizes, propose she get in and go somewhere. Her breath is short. She stops, holding her ground until, jeering at her, they are swept away in the slow traffic.

How could he derive pleasure from something which made her hurt that way? And why afterward didn't he care for her much when she wanted his company more?

She stops. Turns to look. Through the mist and exhaust smoke, headlights continue moving toward her. Kendall Roberts, way back now, is bent to the window of a stopped pickup. He straightens his posture… glances down toward the beach… listens to someone inside. His fists go up, then, and he hops around in a little circle with his head thrown back, crowing over the team's great win.

Under the Clouds

Terry Sanville

I couldn't put it off any longer. I had to ask Dad, and if he refused, I'd have to bug my best friend, Molly. And if she couldn't help…

It took Dewayne McAllister three months to finally ask me to the senior graduation dance. Then at the last minute, in sixth-period Study Hall, he whispered that his jalopy wouldn't start and his parents' car was in the shop. We needed wheels.

I counted myself lucky to be going to the dance at all since Dewayne was good at forgetting things like that. Actually, he was just terminally shy, even with me. But I liked him a lot, ever since sixth grade. Once in Junior High, on the bus ride home, I'd leaned over and offered him my perfectly soft lips to kiss. He just stared at me with those gray-green eyes and smiled. Molly told me once that men know the language of love. For Dewayne, it was like speaking Mongolian.

On Saturday morning my sis Jodie woke me early, excited about going to Hendry's Beach with her girlfriends and wearing her first two-piece swimsuit—not that she had much to show.

"Eggs and bacon?" Mom asked as I slumped into my chair at the kitchen table.

"No thanks. Just a piece of toast."

"You can't survive on that," she scolded.

"I also won't fit into my dress if I eat everything you give me."

"Oh, Clare, you'll be beautiful for the dance."

"Yeah, if a hippo wearing pantyhose is beautiful," Jodie cracked.

"Shut up, Four Eyes."

She glared at me from behind huge horn-rimmed glasses.

"Be nice," Mom said. "You each have positive attributes."

I hated it whenever she said that, as if my body was the subject of some women's magazine's beauty checklist:

☑Hair: soft brown and flowing;

☑Face: expressive—meaning, good for making funny faces;

☑Figure: Rubenesque—meaning, fat.

Jodie squirmed in her seat. "Yeah, ya know, Clare's the stout funny one, right Dad?"

My father had his head buried in the newspaper and wisely grunted something unintelligible. I waited until he put the paper down then sprang it on him.

"Say, Dad, Dewayne was gonna drive us to the dance in his parents' car. But it's in the shop. Do you think we could borrow your—"

"Yeah, sure, honey. Why not."

My mouth fell open.

Mom stopped in mid-stride. "Harold, you won't even let me drive that precious chariot… and now you're gonna let—"

"Gee, thanks, Dad," I said quickly before he could ponder Mom's comment. "Dewayne's a good driver, and I'll make sure he doesn't do anything—"

"Dewayne, do a-n-y-t-h-i-n-g?" Jodie rolled her eyes.

Dad ignored her. "I just thought you'll both be leaving for college soon and… and it's time I trusted you like an adult."

I was prepared to wheedle, beg, cajole, to promise to turtle wax his new '63 Pontiac with three coats. I was ready with my 'I'm a mature young woman' speech. But he'd given in without an argument. I felt cheated, outfoxed, and more than a little wary… because if I was to be treated as an adult, I couldn't wheedle, beg, or cajole anymore, at least not the way I'd perfected as a child. And then there was that whole TRUST thing.

"I'll be home by midnight," I murmured.

"If it's Dewayne, you'll be home a lot sooner than—"

"Shut up, twerp. You know nothing about boys."

"I know plenty."

"That's enough, you two," Mom snapped.

I wolfed down my toast and escaped the breakfast table. Jodie was right. I'd been going with Dewayne all through high school, and we still hadn't… God, it was even embarrassing to say it to myself… hadn't gotten past first base. I may have been Rubenesque, but I knew all about baseball analogies, had listened to Rebecca Stevens whisper excitedly to her girlfriends in fourth period Social Studies about what Tony Spanoza did with her and how far she'd let him go. I had a pretty good idea what 'rounding the bases' was all about. But doing it with shy unassuming Dewayne? And then there was Mom's advice:

"If a boy really loves you, Clare honey, you'll both know it's best to wait."

Jesus peaches, where's the romance in that? Where's the excitement?

After phoning Dewayne with the good news about the car, I spent the afternoon shaving and primping. By dinnertime, I'd used up most of my deodorant pads and wished I were old enough to drink. Maybe Dewayne would sneak a bottle from his father's liquor cabinet? Maybe pigs would fly.

At eight o'clock sharp, our doorbell rang.

"Hey, son, come on in," my Father bellowed. "Clare will be down in a minute."

Dewayne mumbled a reply I couldn't make out. I listened to my folks go through the normal pleasantries then shift to the ever-popular discussion of college. He was going to Berkeley to study engineering. I was going to Northridge to study journalism. Finally, their twenty-question grilling subsided, and I crept down the stairs.

In the hallway mirror, I checked myself out. My new stiletto heels were killing me but looked great. The shimmering gold dress with spaghetti straps and a plunging neckline showed me off to good advantage. I wore my hair down, curling over bare shoulders. If that outfit didn't turn heads, then they were all a bunch of blind morons.

"Wow, you look, like, ya know, really nice," Dewayne said.

"Thank you, and what a beautiful corsage."

He looked blankly at me for a moment, seeming to forget the box clutched between his big hands containing white orchids with maroon striping.

"I… ah, I didn't know what you were wearing. I hope these go okay." He fumbled with the box and, wouldn't you know it, the corsage was one of those wear-on-your-wrist types. God forbid that Dewayne would get anywhere near my breasts to pin one on. He quickly slipped it over my hand. My parents grinned stupidly.

"Well, ah… we gotta get going. Nice talking with you, Mr. and Mrs. Story." He turned to escape.

"Dewayne," my Father called, "you might need these."

Dewayne blushed and reached for the car keys dangling from Dad's outstretched hand. Poor guy, his face was always turning red. But I found it strangely attractive and never made fun of him when it happened.

Once outside in the warm May air, he let out a deep breath and tugged at his paisley necktie. The dark suit looked new. "Jeez, I don't know why I'm so nervous."

"Maybe because this is our last high school dance. But we'll have the whole summer to—"

He slammed the car door on the tail end of my suggestion and dashed around the front of the Pontiac. After fumbling with the keys, we got rolling and slid out onto Los Positas Boulevard under a mackerel sky. Neither of us said anything. But Dewayne kept stealing glances at me with a quiet smile on his face.

We arrived fashionably late, the dance floor already mobbed with couples leaning all over each other. The band wore rose-colored sequined jackets and played a medley of Beach Boys, Ventures, Buddy Holly and Elvis tunes, in a two-fast-ones then one-slow-one sequence. We danced next to Tony and Rebecca. She tapped me on the arm.

"All right, Clare! That's some outfit! You're lookin' good."

"Thanks, Becky. You look great too."

Tony stared at my cleavage and grinned like a Cheshire cat until Rebecca spun him away. Before long I felt perspiration drip down the sides of my face.

"Dewayne, I have to use the powder room. I'll be back in a minute."

"Sure, I'll just, ya know, hang out here."

I left him leaning against the gymnasium's end wall, looking lost but trying to be cool. When he slipped his hands into his pants pockets, his slacks rode up, showing off white sweat socks over dull black loafers. Dewayne was tall, maybe six-two, slender built, with a fair complexion. Only a prominent nose and acne kept him from being anybody's heartthrob, well almost anybody.

When I returned he handed me a cup of punch. All the windows and doors in the gym had been flung open, but the place remained stifling. I grabbed Dewayne's hand and tugged him outside into the courtyard. Couples had secreted themselves into dark corners, talking quietly and making out. We moved to a spot beside a humming Coke machine. He took me in his arms and kissed me full on the lips. I kissed him back. But before we could continue, some fool dropped a quarter in the machine and a soda came thumping down with a loud clunk.

"Ya wanna get outta here?" he whispered in my ear.

"Yeah, sure. Where to?"

"I was thinkin' maybe, ya know, somewhere up off of El Camino Cielo."

"But that's all the way up San Marcos Pass, and the road at night is—"

"I know, I know. But they say the view from on top is fantastic."

"You sure it's the view you're after?"

He stared at me innocently for a moment before breaking into a grin. "Well, ya know, there are all kinds of views."

We clattered across the courtyard and into the parking lot, my heart pounding. When I climbed into the front seat, Dewayne patted the space next to him, and I slid over against his body. He draped a long arm around me. I couldn't stop giggling.

"Easy Clare, we're not even there yet."

"I've been there in my mind plenty of times, Dewayne."

We cruised State Street, with me working the column shifter because I didn't want him to take his arm away. With each shift, I felt the blood rise in my face. A shiver went through me. Dewayne pulled me closer and stroked my arm. I hoped he would do more, but shifting gears got in the way. We turned onto Highway 154, climbed the steep grade and pulled onto the dirt track that crossed the coastal mountains. The Pontiac moved with purpose and determination along the razor-sharp ridgeline toward the Gibraltar Peak overlook.

With both hands on the wheel, Dewayne slid the car into each turn then accelerated out. I felt frightened yet ecstatic. We were near the top. Rounding a tight horseshoe bend, the car plunged into a thick clot of clouds. He jammed on the breaks, and we ground to a halt.

"Jeez, where'd this stuff come from," he croaked.

"I can't see anything. Can you?"

"Nah, uh. Here, let me try the high beams."

He pulled on the switch, but all we saw was thicker gray cotton candy.

"This is like a one-line fog," Dewayne said. "My uncle used to drive a big rig through the San Joaquin. A one-liner means ya only can see one street line out in front of your car."

"I can barely see the front of the car," I said and snuggled next to him. He wore some kind of aftershave with a tangy scent. When I kissed him in back of the ear my lips tingled. He turned and gave me a long French kiss. I could feel his body tighten in my arms. He moaned softly but finally pushed me away, both of us gasping.

"We'd better see about the car," he said and turned off the engine. "Somebody could come along and smack into us."

"I can't have you messing up the cure to my Dad's mid-life crisis."

Dewayne grinned. "My Pop's the same way. Only with him, it's speedboats. Check the glove compartment and see if there's a flashlight."

"Nothing in there but parking tickets. Maybe if you turned the lights out, the moon will be enough."

He clicked them off. It felt like being inside a sock, the darkness almost tactile.

"Why don't we get out and try finding the edge of the road." I slid across, opened the door and lowered my feet. Dewayne's hand clamped around my arm, and I yelped.

"Wait," he hissed.

I perched on the edge of the seat, my legs dangling, while he rummaged in the glove box and came out with a can opener.

"Now be real quiet and listen." He dropped the opener out my door. Only silence, then a soft tinkling from far below followed.

"Holy Jesus," I moaned, staring into the black abyss.

"We'd better sit tight until we can see, don't ya think?"

"Sure Dewayne, whatever you say."

When I slammed the door, my side of the car settled on its springs. I shrieked and slid over against him.

"It's okay baby, just hang on. We'll be able to see in no time." He stroked my hair. I couldn't tell who was trembling more, him or me.

Dewayne snapped on the radio and fumbled with the tuner. From high atop the coastal range, we could pull in almost anything, including Wolfman Jack on XERB from south of the border. I listened to the gravely-voiced DJ and watched the thick clouds slowly lift, forming a pillowy ceiling above us.

"Okay, let's get out my side and see what's up." He pulled on the Pontiac's lights.

"I'm right behind you."

Dewayne pushed the door open and put one foot down, then the other. Turning, he helped me climb out. My stiletto heels sank into the soft dirt, and I almost went ass over teakettle. But he grabbed me and held on. I slipped off my shoes, the sandy soil cold against my pantyhosed feet. As the clouds continued to lift, we checked out the car. It was perched on the shoulder, the right front wheel hanging over the edge and the right rear almost the same.

"Lord, Dewayne, we almost… and my Dad's car…"

"You're right. I don't think we should, ya know, get back in. Looks too dangerous."

I pulled my light shawl tightly around me. It provided no protection against the freshening breeze. Dewayne peeled off his coat and draped it over my shoulders.

"What do you think we should do?" I asked, teeth chattering.

"We could try walking back. But it's gotta be five or six miles to the turnoff, and you'll never make it in those shoes."

"I don't think I've ever walked that far," I said.

"I could leave you here and go for help…"

I looked around at the brooding shapes in the stippled darkness. The glow from a gibbous moon had broken through the cloud cover, showing jagged ridgelines and pools of blackness where the valleys lay. Far below, the lights of Santa Barbara twinkled. It was a fantastic view, but so cold now and forlorn.

"…but I don't wanna leave you," Dewayne continued, "and… and both of us are alone too much already."

I stared into his face. "I don't…"

He slipped his arms around my waist and pulled me to him. We kissed. His hands stroked my back, sliding farther down than before. His kisses left my mouth, descended my neck, and continued down my chest. I moaned and slipped the shoulder straps off. His coat plopped onto the ground. Dewayne nibbled at the fringe of my lacy bra. I reached around to unhook it just as a set of headlights bounced over a rise and charged toward us.

"Ah baby, you're so soft and taste so good, I could—"

"STOP, somebody's coming," I squealed and yanked up my top.

Dewayne barely had time to adjust his pants before a Ford sedan pulled alongside us with a guy and his girl snuggling in the front seat.

"You need some help or are you just here for the view?" The guy gave me a big wink.

"Yeah, my car almost slid off the road," Dewayne answered. "Ya got any chains and could maybe give us a pull?"

"Got some snow chains in the back. We can figure somethin' out."

The guy swung his car around so that it faced ours. In the headlights, they fumbled with the chains but finally got them hooked up. Dewayne climbed in and started the engine. When he released the emergency brake, the Pontiac slipped backward. He stomped on the gas, and the wheels spun furiously. The guy also gunned the Ford in reverse, its tires skittering in the soft dirt. The Pontiac's rear end slowly rotated toward the precipice. I stared at Dewayne sitting grimly in the front seat, his big hands gripping the wheel.

I pictured the chains snapping, Dad's car tumbling end-over-end down the mountain and exploding in flames. I saw Dewayne's parents on their knees, weeping at a gravesite. I relived Dewayne's last caress, the feel of his lips, and that white-hot jolt of electricity that made my whole Rubenesque body quiver.

"DEWAYNE," I screamed.

He stared back, that stupid but lovable grin splitting his face.

The Ford's tires found grip. Slowly the Pontiac righted herself and lumbered onto the road. The air stank with the pungent smell of burning clutches.

The men climbed out of their cars and unhooked the chains.

"All right, you two. Try keepin' it on the road," the guy said before rejoining his date and speeding off.

We sat in the front seat and listened to the Pontiac's muttering engine. I shook for a long time. I think Dewayne did too. Finally, he put the car in gear, and we crept forward until finding a wide spot to pull over.

"Whew, that was—" he began.

"Ye… ye… yeah, I know," I managed.

"Do you want me to take you home?"

The dashboard clock glowed ten-thirty. I remembered the smirk on Jodie's face at the breakfast table. 'Clare's the stout funny one, Clare's the stout funny one,' rattled around my brain like a stuck record. I thought about the years ahead, away from Dewayne's comfortable yet frustrating friendship.

"Yes, please take me home, Dewayne. Tonight, I want to round all the bases and reach home."

I slid next to him and undid as many clasps, snaps, buttons, and bindings as I could. He did the same. We rocked in our cradle under the clouds until the moon went down, the strong scent of our bodies reminding us how young and alive we really were.

Contributors

Elizabeth Abeling

Elizabeth Abeling is a previously unpublished author residing in Pittsburgh, Pennsylvania. She spends most of her time slinging pizzas in an uppity joint Downtown, but when she's not refilling that eighth diet coke, she's bouncing about silly dive bars with her writing group, The Rahnd Table, talking about words and dreams and general nonsense.

Kara Dennison

Kara Dennison is a writer, illustrator, and presenter living in Newport News, VA.

Her work has appeared in anthologies from Titan Books and Obverse books, as well as *Nocturnal Natures* from Zimbell House Publishing and the light novel series "Owl's Flower."

By day, she's a news writer for Crunchyroll.com and a frequenter of the local tea shop. She blogs at karadennison.com and tweets @RubyCosmos

Mike Evis

Mike Evis lives just outside Oxford, England. He is a former software engineer with a long-standing interest in writing – as well as a chronic inability to pass any bookshop without entering and buying a book.

A wide-ranging reader, his interests include modern literature, science fiction, fantasy, and thrillers. He escapes from books by going walking in the Oxfordshire countryside.

He also likes obscure indie music no one has ever heard of. His stories have appeared in a number of anthologies.

Paul Lewellan

For three decades Paul Lewellan taught Creative Writing and coached high school Debate. Eventually, he tired of locker bay duty and retired from public education. Now he teaches Communications Studies at a private liberal arts college in Rock Island, IL.

In the last year, he's published fiction in Old Northwest Review, Firefly Magazine, Black Elephant, and Peacock Journal.

W. P. Osborn

W.P. Osborn's *Seven Tales and Seven Stories* won the 2013 Unboxed Books Prize in Fiction. His short work is in Chicago Quarterly Review, Southern Humanities Review, Texas Review, Hotel Amerika, Mississippi Review, Gettysburg Review, Beloit Fiction Journal, Gargoyle, and other journals.

He retired from teaching at Grand Valley State University in 2016.

You can follow W. P. on his website at: http://www.wposborn.com

Rebecca Redshaw

Rebecca Redshaw is an author and playwright who worked successfully as a specialist in film restoration in Los Angeles for twenty-five years before moving to Pacific Northwest and writing full time.

In addition to extensive articles and short stories published in national newspapers and magazines, she has self-published a novella, *Dear Jennifer* as well as *SOFA CINEMA: An Easy Guide to DVDs, Vol. 1-* a compilation of her published DVD critiques. A theatrical adaptation of *Dear Jennifer* and *FOUR WOMEN*, an original play, have been produced in the United States and Canada.

She was awarded First Prize in the 2009 Lakeview Literary Review for her short story, *Somebody Special.* Currently, she is at work on her fourth novel, *The Girls Go Fishing* and an eighth play. A complete literary vitae can be accessed at www.rebeccaredshaw.com.

Melanie Reitzel

Melanie Reitzel is an RN Lactation Consultant at Stanford Children's Hospital, reminding her patients how to be mammals. She was always in trouble as a kid for sass; in 2012, she earned her MFA in it.

Her work has appeared in Popshot Magazine, ZYZZYVA, Poet Lore, North American Poetry Review, Tulane Review, the Berkeley Poetry Review and in various anthologies.

You can contact Melanie via email at: baddogcafe@aol.com

Terry Sanville

Terry Sanville lives in San Luis Obispo, California with his artist-poet wife (his in-house editor) and one skittery cat (his in-house critic). He writes full time, producing short stories, essays, poems, and novels.

Since 2005, his short stories have been accepted by more than 240 literary and commercial journals, magazines, and anthologies including The Potomac Review, The Bitter Oleander, Shenandoah, and Conclave: A Journal of Character.

He has been nominated twice for a Pushcart Prize for his stories *The Sweeper,* and *The Garage.*

Terry is a retired urban planner and an accomplished jazz and blues guitarist—who once played with a symphony orchestra backing up jazz legend George Shearing.

Joe Sifton

Joe Sifton is a Bristol (UK) based financial advisor. In the late 70s, he formed the short-lived post-punk band Joe Sifton and Sci-Fi Fans. Following the break-up of the group in 1979, he drifted for a while before settling on a successful career in financial services.

He has been married for thirty-five years to Sandra, who he met at one of the early Sci-Fi Fans gigs. Somewhere along the way, his Georgian townhouse has also become a home for three daughters, various cats and dogs, and the occasional rabbit. Fiction is his latest venture.

DJ Tyrer

DJ Tyrer has plenty of those issues that, while tedious in a brief bio such as this, are greedily devoured when they appear in ghostwritten celebrity biographies, is the person behind Atlantean Publishing (which has been going for two decades), was placed second in the 2015 Data Dump Award for Genre Poetry, and was short-listed for the 2015 Carillon 'Let's Be Absurd' Fiction Competition, which was absurd.

To follow DJ Tyrer, his website is located at: http://djtyrer.blogspot.co.uk/

The Atlantean Publishing website is at: http://atlanteanpublishing.blogspot.co.uk/

Maggie Veness

Maggie Veness lives in a small seaside town in New South Wales, Australia. Her quirky, contemporary short fiction has been print-published across several countries in countless literary journals and anthologies.

Maggie's literary influences include Miranda July, Sam Lipsyte, Hilary Mantel, and Kurt Vonnegut.

When she's not writing or reading, she's madly cycling so she can continue to enjoy chocolate and red wine.

Evelyn M. Zimmer

Evelyn Zimmer began her writing career in the second half of her life. While she has always had a love affair with the written word, it wasn't until now that she has had the time to dedicate herself to her passion.

In her spare time, she enjoys various activities with her friends and visiting her family throughout the States.

Several of her short stories have appeared in numerous Zimbell House Publishing anthologies.

She lives in her family home in Michigan with her husband Paul, and the newest addition to their family, a Shih-Tzu named Leo.

A Note from the Publisher

How to Thank a Contributor

Dear Reader,

Everyone at Zimbell House Publishing would like to thank you for reading *Date Night*. If you would like to thank a particular contributor, the best way is to leave a review for them. You may do so by leaving one on our Goodreads page, under the *"Date Night"* title, by using the link below: http://www.goodreads.com/ZimbellHousePublishing and be sure to mention the contributor directly.

Why leave a review? Reviews help budding authors build their credibility in the book industry. By posting a review on Goodreads, you help other readers find new authors they may wish to follow, and you never know, your review may end up on an author's website one day.

★★★★

Social Media Links

Friend us on Goodreads:
https://www.goodreads.com/ZimbellHousePublishing

Visit our website:
http://www.ZimbellHousePublishing.com

Follow us on Twitter:
http://twitter.com/ZimbellHousePub

Other Anthologies from Zimbell House

The Fairy Tale Whisperer

The Mysteries of Suspense

Garden of the Goddesses

Elemental Foundations

Romantic Morsels

The Steam Chronicles

Pagan

Tales from the Grave

The Adventures of Pirates

Curse of the Tomb Seekers

Travelers

Dark Monsters

On a Dark and Snowy Night

Where Cowboys Roam

The Key

Veil of Secrets

Tournament Games

The Lost Door

Nocturnal Natures

It's an Urban Style of Love

The Neighbors

Coming Soon from Zimbell House

Why?

The Mountain Pass

River Tales

Summer Fling: Tales of Seduction

The Witch Games